Praise for *The Shape of Thunder*

IndieNext Selection
Junior Library Guild Selection

"With taut pacing, nuanced characters, and compassionate depictions of grief and trauma, Warga's novel is both timely and transcendent."
—*SLJ* (starred review)

"Moving and beautifully written, *The Shape of Thunder* is an important book that will push readers to consider what they would do in an impossible situation, and how far they would be willing to go to change it."
—*BookPage* (starred review)

"The story builds steadily toward a moving conclusion; Warga's lyrical language and credible rendering of both middle school life and of the tensions of two families coping differently with personal devastation make for a perceptive, sensitively told novel about the effects of gun violence."
—*Publishers Weekly*

"[Cora and Quinn] are well developed, and Warga skillfully handles both their delicate, emotional friendship and larger subjects of grief and gun violence. Powerful and emotionally complex."
—*Kirkus Reviews*

"This will spark meaningful discussions."
—*ALA Booklist*

"Warga skillfully develops unique voices for her narrators, and the novel's alternating-perspective structure works well. Emotions run high throughout the book without dragging down the plot, and the portrayal of middle-school life is utterly authentic."
—*The Horn Book*

"Warga limns a tale that downplays sensationalism while acknowledging the deep fear that many readers may carry regarding school shootings."
—*The Bulletin of the Center for Children's Books*

"A beautiful friendship story about the love that is possible even when the worst has already happened."
—Rebecca Stead, Newbery Medalist

the Shape of Thunder

JASMINE WARGA

BALZER + BRAY

An Imprint of HarperCollinsPublishers

For Lillian Nour and Juniper Lee, who ask big questions

ONE
CORA

I like learning things. Especially about math and science, because they help explain why the world is the way it is. A famous mathematician once said, "Mathematics is the music of reason."

I've always believed that. The best thing about math is that it makes sense. The actual best thing about math is that everything adds up, all neat and in order.

Here's what I know about the number twelve: Twelve is four times three. Twelve is six times two. Twelve is ten plus two. This is all simple math, right? Elementary school stuff. Reason and logic. Twelve is also two less than fourteen.

Fourteen is how old Mabel was when she died.

I am twelve today. Someday in the future I will be more than twelve plus two. I will become older than my older sister.

There is no music in that fact. There is absolutely no reason. It does not add up, all neat and in order.

"You ready, Corrie?" Dad asks as he slips on his navy windbreaker. Grams is standing beside him in her puffy red coat. It's not even that cold outside, and she's been wearing it for ten minutes already. Grams is always ready before everyone else.

"We really don't have to go."

"Of course we do." Dad gives me a smile and I know it's supposed to look encouraging, but I can see the sadness leaking out behind it.

"Don't be silly," Grams says, draping an arm around my shoulder and pulling me close enough to her that I can smell her hair that always smells like lemons. Grams is the only person I know who washes their hair with a bar of soap instead of shampoo. "We always go to Pete's."

This is true. Going to Pete's for birthdays has been a Hamed family tradition for as long as I can remember. We go—all four of us—Grams, Dad, Mabel, and me. We sit in the same back corner booth—the one with saggy cushions—and order chocolate milkshakes and an extra-large pizza. Whoever's birthday it is gets to pick the pizza toppings.

For Mabel's, we'd always get barbecue chicken. Dad usually picks veggie, though I think he only does that because he's always trying to get everyone to eat more vegetables. (When Mabel and I were younger, he printed off a copy of a nutrition guide, circled the vegetable and fruits section, and hung it up on our wall—Mabel let it stay for a day, before ripping it down and replacing it with a picture of a rainbow she'd drawn at school.) Grams usually chooses whatever the monthly special is, and me? I pick cheese. Mabel used to say that cheese was boring, and well, the truth is, I'm a little bit boring.

Boring is okay with me. Boring is safe. Boring is your sister coming home from school like you expect her to.

"What's this?" Grams says. She's been idling on the porch, whereas Dad and I have already made it halfway down the driveway to where Dad's car is parked. She picks up a cardboard box. There's a thick piece of duct tape running diagonally across it to keep it shut. "Sweet pea, it has your name on it. Must be a birthday present."

I give her a confused look. There's no one besides Grams or Dad who would get me a birthday present. Maybe Owen. My stomach flips a little at that thought and then I feel guilty. Now, of all times, it's not right for my body to be doing the new fizzy thing it does when I think of him.

Grams studies the box, holding it out toward me. I know exactly who the box is from the moment I see the chunky handwriting that slopes to the left. A sticky knot forms in my throat.

Grams must recognize the handwriting too because she says, "Oh, it's from Quinn. Did you invite her to come with us to Pete's?" Grams asks. She casts a quick glance toward Quinn's house, which is right next door, like it has always been, even though I've spent the last ten months trying to pretend like it doesn't exist.

I shake my head. I can't bring myself to say words. Grams should know I didn't invite Quinn. I haven't talked to her since that day.

The day Mabel died. November 11.

Dad clears his throat. "You could've invited her."

I know I'm about to get another big lecture from Dad and Grams about how I should still be friends with Quinn McCauley. The conversation always goes the same way: they tell me that I shouldn't hold what Quinn's brother did against her, that Mabel wouldn't want me to punish Quinn.

The thing is, though, deep down, I think Mabel would hold a grudge against Quinn, and she'd expect me to, too.

It's not that my sister was mean or anything, but she was what grown-ups call "a force." When she got mad, she stayed mad. Even about silly, stupid things. She never forgave David Wilkes for breaking the ceramic bird she made in second grade, and she never forgave Addison Taylor for wearing the exact same red glittery dress as her to the eighth-grade end-of-the-year dance.

Mabel wasn't always nice. She got mad a lot. Those two things are facts. You simply can't argue with them.

That's one of the things I hate the most about Mabel

being gone. People want to remember her differently, perfectly. She was Mabel, my sister, my favorite person in the whole world, but she wasn't perfect. I want to remember her as she was. My memory of my sister is a triangle, made up of bold lines but also sharp angles, and everyone else wants to remember her as a boring and simple circle.

I open the car door and slide into the back seat. Grams holds on to the package from Quinn, cradling it in her lap, as Dad steers the car out of the driveway. I keep sneaking glances at the box, wondering what could possibly be inside, even though I don't want to be thinking about it.

I don't want to be thinking about the McCauley family at all.

Outside the car window, the sun is hanging low in the sky, about to slip below the horizon, and it's making a hazy orange trail. We drive by tree-lined streets and manicured postage-stamp–sized lawns where leaves have been raked into neat piles by the curb.

September, my birthday month. It used to mean new school supplies, freshly sharpened pencils and blank notebooks. School used to be a place that was safe. A place where I learned things. But last year, I learned the worst thing: no place is really safe.

So these days when I think of September, I think of it as the time of year when night starts earlier and lasts longer—a darkness that comes and doesn't leave.

Dad steers the car along the road that will lead us to

downtown. Chestnut, my hometown, is one of a collection of small Ohio towns that are along the old railway line, which means we have a little downtown-type square. It's mostly shops and restaurants with one hardware store, and also a new fancy pet-food place that just came in. Grams thinks the pet food place is wild. "People are feeding their dogs more expensive food than I eat!" she says, but the store always seems to be crowded. That's Chestnut for you.

Pete's Pizza is in this downtown square. Dad parks the car and we all get out. He holds the restaurant door open for Grams and me. When I walk through, he says, "Twelve. I can't believe my little girl is twelve. I'm probably going to have to stop calling you my little girl soon, huh?"

I blink the tears away from my eyes before Dad can see them. I have to be strong for him.

I'm the only Hamed girl left.

Dad gently presses his hand into the small of my back. As we walk toward the booth, I look over my shoulder. I spot our car in the front row of the parking lot. In the passenger seat, I can make out the shadowy outline of the cardboard box. The fading sunlight hits it in a way that makes it look like it's winking at me.

I take a deep breath and turn my head away.

TWO
QUINN

Dear Parker,

I only ever saw you cry once.

It was in the woods. It was after you helped me down from the tree.

Do you remember?

Dad always told us not to cry. Especially you.

The time I saw you cry, it wasn't because you were sad.

I haven't cried since it happened, but I'm pretty sure I'm going to cry when I see you again.

Your sister,
Quinn

It's been three days since I put the box on Cora's doorstep, and I still haven't heard anything from her.

The last bell of the day rings, and I jolt toward the library. As I scramble to get there before anyone spots me, I imagine the scene being narrated by one of those voices from the boring documentaries we sometimes watch at school. The kind of voice that speaks in a stiff and funny-sounding way, like: *Quinn McCauley races down the tiled halls in the hopes that none of her classmates will notice her before she has once again disappeared from view.*

"Hi, Quinn," Mrs. Euclid greets me as I walk into the library.

Before last year, I hardly ever went to the school library. Maybe because I've never thought of myself as a great reader or Language Arts student. Whenever I get one of my writing assignments back, there's so much red on it, circling all the things I did wrong, that it looks like it's bleeding. I mean, I think I have okay ideas. But I'm never able to get them down without lots of spelling and grammar mistakes or something else wrong.

I lose track of my thoughts a lot. I have so many of them that by the time it comes to write them down, it ends up coming out all wrong, and my teachers start to think I don't have any thoughts at all.

I'm also never able to memorize facts from books, so I sometimes do badly on reading quizzes. I mean, I could tell you why I liked the book. Or why I didn't. Or how I felt about the characters. But my teachers always want to know things like what color glasses the main character wore, and those are the types of details that slip my mind. Those are also the type of details my brain forgets when I get nervous. And I'm always nervous during quizzes.

Anyway, I didn't think the library was for me. I figured it was only for kids like Cora who are really good at school.

But after last November, I started coming in here all the time. And when school started back up this year, I found myself here again. I've figured out that I kinda love the library. The long line of shelves, the quiet hum of the ceiling fan, and the smell. The library totally smells a certain way. Kind of musty, but also welcoming. It smells like a place where you can belong.

I sit down at a table in the back, and Mrs. Euclid pushes a cart of books toward me.

"We just got a book in that I think you'll like."

"Really?"

Mrs. Euclid smiles, and I notice her bright-colored purple lipstick. Mrs. Euclid is Black and wears her hair in long box braids that almost reach her waist. Today she has on earrings shaped like BB-8 and her shoes are ballet flats that look like mice. Mrs. Euclid always has the best shoes.

"It's on your favorite topic. Time travel!" She reaches down and fishes a book off the cart. She hands it to me.

The cover has a boy standing in the middle of a light tunnel.

"He travels all the way back to the Jurassic era. Pretty cool, huh?"

I turn the book over in my hands. I stare at the boy on the cover, and irritation itches inside me. This boy did what I want to do. Also, for some reason, it's almost always a boy on these type of books. Super annoying.

I point at the cover. "Isn't that kind of a spoiler?"

"How so?"

"Because he's standing in that light tunnel, so we already know that he managed to time-travel. Why should I read the book?"

Mrs. Euclid laughs a little. "I think the book is more about what happens after he time-travels. Not so much about whether or not he is able to."

"Hm." I'm not sure this book will be that useful for my research, but I thank Mrs. Euclid anyway.

I can hear kids talking in the hallway outside the library. Once upon a time, this was my favorite part of the day. School can be tough because it's so much sitting.

But the end of the day was great. It's when I got to see all my friends. Cora has always been my best friend, but I used to have other friends, too. Lots of them, actually. Like Scarlett and Ainsley, who I played soccer with on the weekends, and after our games, we'd beg our parents to take us out for ice cream, and then we'd have a sleepover at Ainsley's house, building massive pillow forts in her basement.

And there was Jacob and Bea and Emerson, we'd all been friends since kindergarten. Last year before it happened, I ate lunch with them every day and then played tetherball with Bea at recess. I was always a better player than Bea, but I sometimes let her win when I knew she was having a bad day.

Now none of those kids talk to me.

They talk about me, sure.

But they don't talk to me.

It's okay, though. I even kind of actually get it. Like they can't look at me and not see what my brother did. And I mean, I can't look at me and not see what Parker did, so I don't really blame any of them. Even though I'd be lying if I said that it doesn't feel like sandpaper scratching my skin every time one of them turns away in the hall, pretending like they don't know me.

But like I said, it's okay.

It's okay because I'm going to fix it.

Mom has this lipstick that's a shade of red called "Leading Lady." Back before everything happened, when Mom still was busy with work, she would wear that lipstick. She said it was a bright spot that could get her through even the toughest and hardest of days. It was a fake-it-until-you-make it sort of thing.

That's how I feel about this plan. You see, whenever I think about Parker, I end up missing him so much I feel sick. I feel sick because what kind of person misses someone who did what Parker did? And then my sickness turns to anger, an anger so hot that I feel like I could spit lava. When my anger gets that hot, I go back to thinking about my plan. And boom. Bright spot. The lava cools down.

It's actually better than a bright spot. It's a changer of spots. It's a fixer, my plan.

I call it my plan, but really it's Cora's. She's the one who has always been interested in time travel. That's how I came up with this whole thing.

One night, I was sitting at the computer, listening to Mom and Dad argue about the things that they keep promising to one another that they won't argue about in front of me (money, the guns, everything with Parker) and I didn't want to listen to them anymore, so I distracted myself by clicking on random article after random article.

Mom teases me that I turn into a zombie when I'm on the computer, clicking from one thing to another. I used to find that joke funny, but then Parker actually did become infected by things on the internet, and when I think about that, I get that lava-vomiting feeling again.

Anyway, I don't really know how I found the article. Maybe I was missing Cora, and somehow that led me there. I saw the headline, and it seemed like something she might be interested in, so I clicked on it, even though I knew I wouldn't understand all the science-y language. I clicked on it because I hoped that reading it would make me feel like I was talking to her again.

Even with all the science-y language, I was able to understand a few things. I was able to understand that a very smart scientist who worked at one of those super-famous schools, the type of school that Cora talks about wanting to go to for college, was saying that time travel was possible. He used all these other strange words like *wormholes* and *fabric of our universe* and *light speed*, but what stuck with me was the word *possible*.

Even a girl like me who doesn't understand a lot of science-y terms knows what *possible* means.

Possible means it's real.

Possible means it could happen.

I remember in fourth grade, my teacher, Mrs. Banks, told us about this old guy in ancient Greece named Archimedes who shouted "Eureka!" in the bathtub when he figured out the answer to a really tough math problem. Since I'm never the one who figures out the really tough math problem, that story was sort of lost on me, but as I read this interview with this very smart scientist, I whispered, "Eureka."

This was it.

This was the solution.

Time travel was possible, and I was going to do it. I wish

I could say that I started my research that night. But I didn't. That all came later.

Instead, I ran to the corkboard in my room, where I keep old photos of Cora and me. My corkboard is a collection of things that I love. On it, I've pinned a small poster of the US women's soccer team, the menu from my favorite hamburger place, a picture of my soccer team from last year, and one of me with my mom on a beach in North Carolina when we were visiting Gammie and Papa. I used to have a photo of my whole family, but I took it down last November. I couldn't stand to look at my brother's face.

And the rest of my corkboard is filled with photos of Cora and me. Even after it happened, even after Cora stopped talking to me, I didn't take down any of the pictures. There are photos of us at all ages, including what I think is the first picture of us ever. It's from Cora's birthday party when she turned two. That was her first birthday after her mom left.

I never met her mom. Or if I did, I don't remember. I don't remember the party either, but I've always loved this picture because it proves that Cora and me go way back. I would look at it whenever I felt moody that she was spending so much time after school with the Talented and Gifted club or wasn't able to eat lunch with me because she'd been invited to a special pizza party that was only for kids who got an A on the math test. It helped remind me that she

14

really was my best friend. My best friend since forever.

In the photo, my face is smeared with chocolate cake, and my white freckled arms are squeezing Cora's waist. Cora's smiling perfectly for the camera, and there isn't even a speck of chocolate icing around her lips. While my striped purple shirt has sloppy brown splotches all over it, her pink dress is completely unstained. My light red hair was already long, falling in front of my face in a tangled mess. Cora's hair hadn't come in all the way yet, but you could already tell that it was going to be thick and curly like her dad's. She has his same dark olive skin tone, too. Grams has always said that Cora's golden-hazel eyes come from her mom, but I'm not sure. I just know that her and Mabel had the same eyes. Cora was always proud of that.

After last November, looking at that photo felt like pressing on a bruise. I would see it and it would remind me of everything that was lost.

But that night, after I read the article about time travel, I saw potential when I looked at that photo. I saw the word *possible*.

Maybe Cora and I had become friends for this very reason. Because we were meant to fix everything.

"Eureka," I repeated, staring at our two-year-old faces.

THREE

CORA

We're supposed to be memorizing state capitals, but Mia and Owen are busy arguing about Junior Quiz Bowl strategy. Mia thinks it's best to always reach for the buzzer, even if you only have a vague idea of the answer. Owen thinks you shouldn't hit the buzzer unless you're more confident.

"What do you think?" Mia says, leaning over toward me. I'm sitting between the two of them, pretending to be completely engrossed in the map of the United States that's in front of me. Really, I'm pretending not to be thinking about what could be inside the box from Quinn McCauley that's sitting upstairs at my house.

I shrug, trying to forget about the box. But I can't. "I think you're both wrong. You only hit the buzzer if you're going to get the answer right."

"That's what I'm saying!" Owen holds his hand out for a high five.

16

I shake my head. "No. You said if you feel more confident. I'm saying, I only want people who always know the answer." I give both him and Mia a teasing smile.

"Ugh!" Mia says, poking me right in the ribs. "You are seriously annoying."

I shrug again. "I just like to win."

"Okay," Owen says, snatching the map of the United States from me. "So what's the capital of Vermont?"

I was literally just staring at the New England states, but my brain goes mushy. When I try to picture the image of Vermont, all I see is the outline of the unopened box from Quinn. Not helpful.

"Um—"

"Montpelier," Mia interjects.

"Ding, ding!" Owen says.

Mia is admittedly better at state capitals, but I still think I'm a little better of a Quiz Bowl player overall. I'm more well-rounded in my trivia knowledge. Or that is, I was a better player until today. Today, I can't focus at all.

Quiz Bowl is new this year. Even though our school is for grades five through eight, only grades seven and up are allowed to join sports teams. Quiz Bowl is a sports team. To participate, you have to get a physical. This made Dad and Grams laugh and laugh, but I took my blood pressure results seriously.

Quiz Bowl practice takes place in Coach Pearlman's room. Or rather, Mr. Pearlman. He's Mr. Pearlman when he's my science teacher during sixth bell. He's Coach Pearlman when we meet after school for Quiz Bowl.

We practice twice a week and compete once a week in meets against other local schools. If we have a winning season, we'll qualify for the regional playoffs, and if we do well in the regional playoffs, we'll make it to state. That's the goal.

The questions at the meets vary from presidential history to wildlife biology to state capitals to solving mathematical equations. It's basically one big mix of nerdy trivia, and I'm 100 percent here for it.

"I hope the noise I'm hearing over there is the sound of future glory and not fooling around," Coach Pearlman says, looking up from his desk, where he's grading science quizzes. I resist the urge to ask if he's gotten to mine yet. I'm worried that I might have gotten question number three wrong, but I feel good about the rest of the quiz.

"We're state-capital experts," Mia assures him.

Coach Pearlman twirls his pen between his fingers. "Good, because I don't want another Birmingham-Montgomery mix-up."

Owen's face flushes. That was his mistake at our first meet of the year, but it just as easily could've been mine.

"We're on it," I say, and give Owen a reassuring smile.

There are seven members on the Quiz Bowl team. We're a small but mighty bunch. A team, yeah, but we're also competitive with one another because only three of us get to play at a time.

"Coach is just teasing you because you're a good player and he knows you can take it," I tell Owen.

"That and you royally messed up," Mia teases. She tugs at the sleeves of her T-shirt. It's made from this recyclable material that looks scratchy, but she keeps insisting it isn't. Her squirming tells another story, though. Mia's new thing this school year is she is only going to wear clothes that are sustainable. She also announced that she's only going to wear natural deodorant, which, okay, cool, but I really didn't need to know that. There's only so much time you want to spend thinking about your friend's armpits.

"Owen's still the best there is at remembering the election year for all the presidents," I say.

Mia gives me a funny look, her sharp blue eyes narrowing in a way that makes me think she knows my secret. The secret being that sometimes when I'm around Owen these days my stomach feels like a soda can that someone shook up. That's another thing that's new since summer.

"You're right," Mia finally says, and I let out a shallow breath of relief. If she knows at least she didn't say anything in front of him.

"So how was your birthday?" Owen asks. He taps his new red Converse sneakers. Owen's really into indie rock bands whose lead singers all wear Converse sneakers. His record collection is growing. Who even has a record player? Well, Owen does. He bought one at a garage sale last year.

The record collecting is a hobby that I don't understand, but I wish I did. I even asked Grams to buy me a T-shirt of one of the bands he likes. It came in the mail a few weeks ago, but I haven't worn it yet. I'm worried he'll notice if I do. Or I'm worried he won't notice. I don't know.

Owen's cool in a way that Mia and I definitely aren't. He's never mean about it, but people just like Owen. Mia and me are more of what Grams calls "an acquired taste."

We've all been friends since second grade, when we got grouped together for a project about caterpillars. We made an awesome papier-mâché cocoon. Over the past couple of years, Mia and I have stayed hopelessly nerdy, and Owen has gotten, well, cooler. He has all these new friends that he talks about concerts and music blogs with. I was actually nervous he wouldn't do Quiz Bowl, but I was glad when he proved he's still got a lot of nerd left in him, too.

I grab the map back from him and stare at it again. "Uh, my birthday? It was fine. I didn't really do anything."

That's my way of trying to tell them that it's not like I didn't invite them to my party. I just didn't have one. I know a long time ago they used to get jealous that I only invited Quinn to come with my family to Pete's. But things with Quinn were different. She wasn't a school friend. She was—

Well, it doesn't matter. Things are different in a different way now.

"Man, I love my birthday," Owen says.

"Me too," Mia adds. "Especially the cake."

"The presents and the cake are great, obviously, but the best part is it's the one day of the year that Mom and Dad pay more attention to me than Erika."

"Oh, please, I'm sure it's not the only day of the year," I say.

Owen's face is serious. "You don't even know. They SPOIL Erika. She gets away with everything."

Erika is Owen's adorable younger sister. She's in third grade, wears polka-dot everything, and everyone loves her.

"That's because she's the youngest," Mia says. "My two brothers get away with everything, too. But, hey, I'm going over to the eighth-grade table for a second. It looks like Peter has an updated list of practice questions."

Owen and I share a smile. Only Mia would be that thirsty to see new practice questions. We watch as she quietly tiptoes toward Peter. Technically, we're all one team, but since we're younger, we all are still definitely intimidated by the eighth graders. Even if we won't admit it aloud.

"For what it's worth, I don't get the impression that your parents like Erika better. Look, the bulletin board in your parents' office is full of your schoolwork, not Erika's."

Owen's mom, Dr. Tanaka, is my dentist. His dad is also a dentist. They run a practice together. I think it's really cute that his parents are so proud of his perfect quizzes that they hang them up. I always look at them while I wait to get called for my teeth cleaning.

"That's because I get better grades!"

I give him a look. "I think it's because you're the oldest."

"You don't understand how much they spoil Erika Sakura."

Both Owen and Erika have their first names, and then what they call their Japanese names, which are also their middle names. They use their middle names at home and when they visit their family in Japan. Owen's is Daisuke. He shared that with me in third grade. It made me feel special to know it.

"Okay, kids," Coach Pearlman says, standing up from behind his desk. Coach Pearlman is white and tall and broad-shouldered and has a completely bald head except for two wisps of gray hair. He looks like someone who might be the football coach instead of the Quiz Bowl one. "I know today was more of a free-for-all practice, but on Thursday, we're going to do a scrimmage. Once I see how you all perform in the scrimmage, I'll get a better sense of a good game plan for our next meet. Sound good?"

We all nod. I sneak a glance at Mia, who is very happy to be sitting with the eighth graders. She's paging through the new practice questions.

Coach Pearlman gives us each a high five on our way out the door. Mia, Owen, and I cluster back together once we're in the hallway. Owen and Mia go back to arguing about buzzer strategy as we head toward our lockers. It's only when they stop talking all of a sudden that I realize something is going on.

That's when I see Quinn McCauley standing right in front of my locker.

Mia looks at me. We've never talked about what went wrong with Quinn and me. There wasn't much to say. It was an equation where x was really, really obvious.

"We'll see you tomorrow?" Mia asks.

"No," I say, shaking my head. "I just need to get my math textbook, and then I'll walk outside with you guys."

I don't look at Quinn when I say this, but I step closer to my locker, hoping she'll move out of the way. When I glance up, she's still standing there. She's wearing a navy-blue hoodie and jeans, and her long red hair is partially obscuring her face. When we were younger, Grams used to constantly tell her to push back her hair or she was going to get sties in her eyes. Quinn and I would laugh whenever Grams said that because of the rhyme. "Sties in your eyes," we'd sing together as we walked into kindergarten. We were probably really annoying, but it was hilarious when we were five.

My throat is dry when I open my mouth to speak. "Could you please move?"

Quinn's eyes meet mine. I flinch and break eye contact, but I hear her sneakers squeaking against the floor.

"Cora," she says. "Did you get . . . ?" She trails off.

When she was younger, Quinn was in speech therapy. She would stutter and she wasn't always able to fully complete sentences. It mostly went away as she got older, but it still happens sometimes. We developed a code where I would blink at her to see if her brain was doing what she called a "freeze-up."

Without thinking, I turn and blink at her.

She blinks back. Twice. That means *Yes, but I'm okay.*

I push past her, and she steps out of the way to let me in. I fiddle with my locker, my hands shaking. I mess up the combination once but get it right on the second try. I grab my math book and place it in my backpack. I open my planner and do a quick check that I don't need anything else.

When I shut my locker, Quinn says, "Cora, did you open the box? Did you see? I've found a way to fix things."

I turn around to face her. Blood rushes to my face. The whole hallway tilts on its axis. I feel like I'm upside down. "Fix?" I say. "How dare you even say that? There's absolutely nothing that could fix what your brother did. I'm sorry, Quinn, but I can't talk to you. Not now. Not ever."

Mia and Owen are waiting for me at the end of the hallway. I'm not sure how much of this conversation they've heard. Hopefully not any of it.

"Please, Cora!" Quinn shouts out. Her voice echoes against the lockers. "It's time travel. You know all about it. It's—it's—it's . . ."

She doesn't complete the sentence, and I don't turn around. But even though I don't turn around, the words *time travel* knot inside me. What is she talking about? A staticky feeling tingles in the tips of my fingers. I shove my hands into my pockets, trying to ignore it, but it lingers.

I jog to catch up with Mia and Owen. When I reach them, Mia's lips are a straight, pursed line, and Owen's awkwardly shuffling his feet.

"Are you okay?" Mia asks.

I shake my head. "I don't want to talk about it."

Mia's lips stay pursed. We all stand there for a couple seconds. Mia keeps looking at me like I'm a math problem with a remainder that she's not sure what to do with.

Finally, I raise my hand in a little wave. "Well, I'll see you guys tomorrow." I peel away from the group to walk toward Grams, who I spot waiting for me in the parking lot, that tingly feeling still in my fingertips. *Time travel.*

FOUR
QUINN

Dear Parker,

Did you know Mom and Dad fight all the time now? I know when you were around they used to argue, but that was normal parent type stuff, right? Like Mom getting mad that Dad forgot to sign my permission slip or Dad getting annoyed that Mom put the empty cereal box back in the cabinet instead of tossing it out.

Now they argue about you. And why you did what you did. Everyone says it was Mom and Dad's fault. Mom's mad about Dad's guns, and I get that.

Honestly, deep down, I know it wasn't Mom's or even Dad's fault. I don't think they knew anything.

But I did. That one afternoon, I saw you.

I should've said something, but I didn't.

Your sister,
Quinn

Talking with Cora did not go the way I wanted it to. But at least I know that Cora hasn't opened the box. Maybe now she will because she'll be curious. As mad as Cora is, I also know she's never been able to resist a good mystery.

I'm counting on that.

I push open the door and head out of school. Our school backs up to a large forest preserve. The forest preserve runs across the width of the whole town. Which means that I can cut through the woods to get home. Technically, we're not supposed to do that. We're supposed to walk the long way on the sidewalk. And I always followed those rules until last year, and then the rules didn't seem that important.

As I walk deeper into the woods, the rest of the world starts to fade away. The trees stretch up high above me, shading most of the sky. Their leaves are still mostly green, but some of them are starting to turn orange or burnt golden at the edges. The outside air smells like campfire smoke and cinnamon.

It's the type of scene that I would like to draw, but haven't ever been able to. An explosion of colors and textures. I can draw figures and shapes okay, but I can never nail down the other stuff, the stuff that makes a place alive. The smells, the odd angle of light splashing on the forest ground, the stillness.

The stillness is really hard to draw. But it's also one of the things I love most about the woods, how quiet they are.

I come to the woods because I'm looking for my brother. When I'm in the woods, I can pretend I'm in another world. I am looking for Parker from before, the person he was when we were younger, the person I want to save. My brother does not deserve to be saved after what he did, but I can't help wanting to save him anyway. My desire to save him is a panicky itch that I can't stop scratching.

All the things about time travel that I've read online say that if you want to time-travel, you have to find a wormhole. I'm sure Cora would have a more scientific definition, but the way I understand it is that a wormhole is like a door to another part of time. You can use a wormhole to go forward or backward.

I want to go backward. I need to go backward.

The good news is all my Google searching has told me that going backward is easier than going forward. But finding a wormhole is not easy, even if you are going backward. Whenever I read about how hard it is to find a wormhole, I start skipping over words and my brain feels overwhelmed.

Because of my word-skipping brain, I'm going to need Cora's help when it comes to all the complicated stuff like how to build a time machine, but I was able to understand the part that said wormholes are most likely to be found in ancient places. Places with memory.

I'm pretty sure the woods are an ancient place. And the woods hold so many memories for me. Memories of him.

Everything I've read says the best way to find a worm hole is to ask for one to appear. That makes me think of magic. I imagine myself like a witch, looking for the perfect place to cast a spell. I might not be able to build the time machine without Cora's help, but I'm determined to find the best spot to build one.

And that is something I can do because I know the woods. I know their magic.

Every day on my walk home, I scan the forest, searching for something that stands out to me. Something that says: *This is the place. This is where something magical could happen.*

And every day, I keep coming back to this one giant oak tree. The tree calls me toward it, echoing with the memory of my brother, reminding me of the person he was before he became the type of person who could do what he did.

I keep resisting it, this tree. It is a tree with history. And history is the past and the past is a monster lurking in the shadows. That monster is big and mean and scary and I don't want to face it.

But I know I have to.

The tree grows right at the bank of the creek that splits the forest preserve in two. In order to reach it, I have to cross the creek. Crossing today should be easy since the water in the creek is low because it hasn't rained for a week. Sometimes the current of the creek grows to a loud *whoosh*, but right now it's barely a gurgle.

Hopping from rock to rock, I cross over to the other side. I don't even get my sneakers wet. That has to be a good sign. These days I'm always looking for signs.

The giant oak tree has thick branches that stick out in every direction. It looks like the type of tree you would find on the cover of a fantasy book from the library. It's easy to picture an illustration of it, lots of heavy charcoal shading, two witches flanking the tree, a big fat full moon in the sky.

When we were younger, Parker and I played in the woods together all the time. We'd run in so far in that I'd wonder if we'd ever be able to find our way home. But back then, Parker always led me home.

Because he was older, he was a little better at climbing trees. I was faster, but he could get higher. One day, he struggled to climb up the giant oak tree. He only made it a few branches before slowly trekking back down.

"Don't climb that one," he told me. "It's too tall."

I ignored him. Struggling, I pulled myself up onto one of the bottom branches. From there, I was able to scramble toward the top. It was only when I got very high that I realized my mistake. Staring down at the ground, a fear spread through me.

"Help!" I screamed down to him.

And my brother came. He climbed the tree. Slowly. And slowly again, he helped me down. I squeezed his hand the whole way. When my feet touched the ground, I saw the tears in his eyes.

"You're okay," he said. "You're okay. You're okay, right?" He wiped his eyes to hide his tears, but I saw them. They meant something to me. Something good. Something real. I wish I had told him that he didn't have to hide them.

"I'm not okay," I say to the woods. To the emptiness around me. This time there are no tears. There's only me and my memories.

My memories of my brother are like a garden full of weeds. I pull at them, somedays wanting to remove the bad ones, somedays wanting to remove the good ones because they hurt even more. I've pulled out this memory so many times, but it keeps growing back.

I press my palm against the rough bark of the giant oak tree and close my eyes. "Please," I whisper to it. "Please be the right place. Help me fix things."

A tiny part of me expects the tree to answer me, but it doesn't. A gust of wind ripples through the forest, rustling the tree's leaves and lifting up the back of my hoodie.

But that feels like enough of an answer.

FIVE
CORA

"You know it won't bite," Grams says as I'm tapping my pencil against my uncompleted math homework. I've been staring at the same problem for five minutes.

Dad's in the kitchen cooking. It's his night for dinner. Dad is not a great cook, but he's mastered cheesy scrambled eggs. His trick is to add lots of generous pinches of salt. For accuracy's sake, it should be noted that his pinches of salt are more like handfuls. We all have to drink a lot of water on Dad's dinner nights.

Grams is knitting in the living room. Or at least I thought she was knitting. Now I get the sense that she's spying on me while I struggle to solve for x. Grams has always been a grade-A sleuth.

I sigh and sit down on the floor. I've been on my knees for the past hour. I like to do my homework around the coffee table, but that means kneeling. Mabel always thought that was strange, but it works for me.

"I'm talking about the box," Grams says.

I grip my pencil. "I know."

"You could open it before dinner."

I sigh again. This time in a louder and more dramatic way.

Grams doesn't seem to get the message, though. She just keeps on knitting. She's working on a cream-colored cardigan for herself right now. Before Mabel died, she was working on a pullover that Mabel had picked out. It was teal and gray with a chevron pattern. It was only half-finished when we got the news. I don't know what happened to it, but sometimes when I see Grams knitting I think about that sweater that's probably collecting dust in the back of her closet, and it makes me want to cry.

"It can be easier to just set things down, you know," Grams says.

"I don't know what that means. I'm not holding anything up."

Grams gives me a look. "Oh, really?"

I hold out both my hands as if to show her.

"I'm speaking metaphorically, sweet pea."

"I know," I grumble. Metaphors are a concept I understand, but they can be a highly annoying thing when used in an actual conversation.

"Then why are you being so smart?"

"Because I wish you'd let it go."

"Let it go. Hm." Grams gives me her got-you smile. "I think it would help both of us to let it go if you opened the box. As I keep telling you, it's only a box, Cora London."

My middle name was chosen by my mom. My mother gave both Mabel and me middle names of cities that she wanted to someday visit—Paris and London. I don't know if my mother has ever been, but when I was five, Mabel and I pinkie-promised that we'd go visit those cities together when we got older.

Now, because of Quinn's brother, Mabel's never going to be able to visit those cities.

I'm definitely not opening that box.

"Dinner's ready," Dad calls out. He steps out into the living room. He's wearing what Mabel and I called his "Professor's Coat" because it's tweed with elbow patches. He swiftly corrected us that it would more appropriately be called a jacket than a coat, which for some reason made us burst out laughing. "Jacket," Mabel would say for weeks after, and I would answer, "Coat!" and then we'd erupt into giggles all over again.

I instinctively wrap my arms around my stomach, feeling the memory of that laughter in my gut.

"You okay?" Dad asks.

Grams answers for me. "Cora's heading up to her room

34

real quick to check on something. I'll put her plate in the oven to keep it warm."

Dad looks unsure. I glare at Grams.

"Scrambled eggs don't go in the oven," I say.

"Oh, just watch. My old bones will find a way to keep your dinner warm."

I cross my arms over my chest. "I'm not going upstairs."

Dad steps back into the kitchen. He doesn't like to get in the middle of my fights with Grams. She and I don't have that many fights, but back in the day, Mabel and her used to have a bunch of what Grams calls "howlers."

"Cora, baby." Grams's tone is gentler now. "Everyone in this house will feel better if you get it over with."

I can feel hot tears pricking at my eyes. I pat them away with the back of my hand, embarrassed. This of all things should not be making me cry "There's nothing to get over."

Grams raises her chin. "Open the box."

I'm about to argue some more, but I can tell from the glint in Grams's eyes that's she's already five steps ahead of me. Sometimes you can tell you've lost way before a game has been played out.

I move toward the staircase. Grams put the box right beside my bed yesterday. It's been staring me down ever since. See? She's a chess master.

I rest my weight back against the banister, but don't walk up the stairs yet.

Grams keeps eyeing me. She smiles a little. "I'll toast up an extra slice of bread for you."

"My eggs will be cold."

"Nonsense. I told you already, I'll make sure they stay warm."

"Still."

"Cora London, go open the box."

"I'm going to open it, look inside, and then toss everything away."

"Whatever you want as long as you open it."

As I clomp up the stairs, Grams calls up after me, "I'm proud of you, sweet pea."

SIX
QUINN

Dear Parker,

Do you remember when we were little and you looked out the car window and asked Dad what a cement truck was? You wanted to know why it kept turning.

He gave you some explanation about how it has to turn to keep the cement wet so it'll be ready to pour, but you still kept asking that same question. It's like the answer he had wasn't the one you were looking for.

I sort of feel that way now. I keep asking myself all the same questions about you. Even though I know the answers, I keep asking, hoping the answers will change.

Your sister,
Quinn

Dad and Mom were both accountants, but Mom quit her job right after it all happened. So now she's home all the time. She says she's taking time to figure things out. What those things are, she never says.

When I get home, Mom's bouncing around the kitchen. Joni Mitchell is playing softly, and there's a pot on every burner of the stove. I hum along to the song. It's one that Mom and I used to sing together a lot when I was little.

During the time when my Freeze-Ups were the worst, singing helped to get my mind unstuck. My brain doesn't do that so much anymore, but there's still something about singing that makes me feel better.

Mom's wearing a checkered apron, and her hair that's the same red color as mine falls in a long braid down her back. Parker had the same brown hair as Dad, a dark shade that lightened up in the summer. But Mom and I match. She used to say we had "daybreak hair." She hasn't told me that in a while.

"Quinn!" she says. She gives me a tight squeeze. She smells like the entire spice cabinet. Since quitting her job, Mom has gotten really into cooking. Dinner used to be microwaved macaroni and cheese and leftover turkey sandwiches. Now it's things like coq au vin, which I can't quite pronounce.

"How was your day?"

"Fine," I say, and hang my backpack up on the mudroom

hook. Before, I would toss my stuff everywhere. But now I feel like I have to do everything right. I keep hoping that if I do everything as perfectly as I can, the universe is going to reward me with a wormhole.

Please, please, please, I whisper to the universe about a million times a day. *Watch me be a good daughter. Watch me pay attention in class even though it's so hard to sit still. Watch me fold my laundry instead of throwing it into my dresser in one big messy clump.*

"Lots of homework?"

"Not too bad."

Cupcake slinks into the room. She rubs against my legs. Purring loudly as usual. Cupcake was Parker's cat, but she became my cat long before Parker was gone. She became my cat when Parker stopped caring about her and everything else that used to matter to him.

She's gray with white paws. I bend over to scratch Cupcake between her ears. She purrs louder.

Mom holds a wooden spoon out to me. "Here, taste this."

It's a creamy sauce. Lots of garlic. "Yum."

"Good? I messed it up earlier today, but I think I might've gotten it right this time." Mom's eyes are wide. She gets like this a lot recently. If I were to draw her, I'd make her part hurricane, stormy winds with lots of frantic energy.

"It's really good, Mom," I assure her.

She glances over her shoulder at the clock. "Your dad promised he'd be home today in time for dinner."

While Mom quit her job, Dad seems to spend as much time as he can at work. I haven't seen my dad in anything other than a collared shirt, slacks, and a tie since it all happened. If I were to draw Dad, I'd draw him like a cash register, collecting money and slamming shut as fast as he can.

Mom goes back to stirring the various pots and checking whatever's in the oven. "So tell me about your day?"

What she means is: *Reassure me that you're not turning into someone I need to be worried about.*

"It was fine," I say. *Translation: You don't need to worry about me.*

Mom comes back over with another wooden spoon. "Taste this one?"

More garlic. Also delicious. "Yum," I say again.

"Really?"

My lips twist, my mouth opening and shutting. I want so badly to tell her about my plan, about how I'm going to make everything okay again. But I can't. Not yet.

I give her the most reassuring smile I can muster. "It really is, Mom."

SEVEN
CORA

"You sure you don't want to come?" Mia asks. She's leaning against my locker, fingering the ends of her sandy-blond hair. She cut most of it off a week ago—she had some environmental reason for cutting it all off, but I can't remember it now. There are still patches of sunburn on her white skin, left over from her summer trip to Florida where she refused to wear SPF because it's bad for the coral. It looks like it might still hurt, too.

"I can't." I zip up my backpack and sling it over my shoulder.

"Owen's going to be there."

I knit my eyebrows together. "What's that supposed to mean?"

"You know." Mia shifts, her face reddening. I feel my own cheeks warming, too.

"No, I don't."

Mia crosses her arms. "Oh, come on. I thought you'd be excited to know he was choosing us over the music crew."

Mia calls Owen's other friends "the music crew." Only some of them play an instrument, but all of them talk about music so much you'd think it's the only thing in the world that exists. I listen to the public radio station with Dad, so I know how to talk about classical music and fundraising. That means I'm not exactly the best at conversations with Owen's other friends. I'm trying to learn, though.

"It's not like that," I say, refusing to even acknowledge that shaken-up soda can feeling I get sometimes when I see Owen.

Mabel used to ask me all the time if I had a "crush" on someone. She always made it clear that she'd be cool with me liking anyone, regardless of gender, but I could never come up with a single name. I even considered making someone up because I knew she was disappointed that every time she asked, I came up blank.

Back then, the word *crush* felt as foreign and baffling as *exoskeleton* or *deciduous*—the types of words that showed up on spelling quizzes. Even though I could define it, I didn't really understand it. Now that I finally do, I wish more than anything that I could talk to Mabel about it. She would know what to do about the fizzy feeling in my stomach. She would probably also know about the bands Owen likes. She would have good advice.

There should be a word for when you miss a person in the future. Not just missing memories of them, but missing memories you never got to have with them.

Mia must see something in my face. "You okay?"

"Yeah, I'm fine." I close my locker. "I just can't stay late today."

"Well, we'll be in the computer lab if you change your mind," Mia finally says.

Her and Owen are staying after school to "study" for Quiz Bowl. Studying is basically doing a deep dive on fact websites. They'll memorize as many random trivia facts as they can. I should join them, but I can't. I have to find Quinn.

Which is something I never thought in a million years I would be thinking. It is also definitely not something I can tell Mia without being asked tons of questions that I don't want to answer. Or rather, that I can't answer because I don't know how to.

So I'm not exactly lying to her. But I'm also not telling her the truth. The quasi-lie makes my stomach cramp. I detest lying and false information in all its forms.

"See you," I say as we part ways, her heading into the computer lab and me heading—well, I don't know where I'm heading. I walk by Quinn's locker.

She's not there.

I aimlessly stroll down the hallways. She's nowhere to be found. I tilt my head back and sigh. She probably already walked home. Quinn has always been a walker because both of her parents work. We used to walk home together a lot, but I also got picked up by Grams, especially if it was a day when I had something after school.

I head down the sidewalk that winds away from our school toward the athletic fields. I tug on my backpack straps and practice what I'm going to say to Quinn when I eventually find her.

We can't talk about your idea because we're not friends anymore.

We can't be friends anymore because of what happened.

I want what was in the box to be real, but I don't think it is.

But even as I practice saying those things, another voice in my head hisses at me. It's the voice that I'm finding it harder and harder to ignore. It's the voice that has me out here looking for Quinn instead of being in the computer lab practicing for Quiz Bowl.

"Cora?"

I stop walking. It's Quinn. Back when I was younger, I used to think that Quinn and I had the ability to psychically communicate. I'd read a book about best friends who could talk telepathically, and I became convinced that Quinn and I could do that.

That book was fiction, though. Psychic communication is not a phenomenon that checks out under rigorous scientific scrutiny. So I know I didn't just psychically conjure her, but it feels like I did.

I tug hard on my backpack straps again. It feels good to hold on to something. "I was looking for you."

Quinn's face opens like an envelope, a whole letter of feelings spilling out over her face. "You were?"

I turn at the sound of a whistle. The girls' soccer team stampedes across the field. They're doing a drill involving plastic orange cones. I glance at the field and then back at Quinn. "What are you doing here?"

She's looking out at the soccer field, too. "What?"

"Why are you here?" I ask again. "You're not on the team."

"Oh," she says, hanging her head. "I know. I just miss soccer sometimes."

"You could've tried out."

She looks up. "Wait. You know that I'm not on the team?"

I shrug, a little unsure how to answer that. I guess I do know she's not on the team. I'm not sure why. I've tried my best to ignore everything about Quinn McCauley this year, but my brain has registered pieces of information here and there. "You always said you couldn't wait for seventh grade."

"Because that's when team sports start," she finishes my thought. I exhale at the familiarity of it, but then I think of Mabel. This isn't right. I shouldn't feel like this. I grit my teeth. Now isn't the time for exhaling.

"You opened the box," Quinn says.

I nod. I'd planned—I really, really had planned—to open it quickly so I could tell Grams that I did and then toss everything away, leaving it in the garbage to rot. That was before I saw what was in the box, though.

When I'd pulled the first article out of the box and read the headline: "Man in Colorado Claims to Be Time Traveler; Passes Lie Detector Test to Prove It"—my breath got caught in my throat.

I couldn't throw that away without reading it. So I did. The article described a man named Roger Billows who claimed to have traveled from the year 2034 in an attempt to change his son's fate. I kept holding my breath. *Change his son's fate.* I read the article over and over again. It was short, only a couple of paragraphs. Nowhere in the article did it say exactly what had happened to Roger's son.

More importantly, it didn't say whether Roger was successful in saving his son.

Most importantly, it didn't say how Roger managed to actually time-travel.

I kept reading the article, though. I stared at the black-and-white photograph of Roger. In it, he was wearing a pretty basic-looking T-shirt. I wasn't sure what I expected a shirt from 2034 to look like, but this wasn't it. I hoped it was a shirt the cops had given to him. That would answer my doubts, at least.

After I read that first article, I couldn't help myself from reading the whole stack. I never ended up coming back down for dinner, but Grams didn't bug me. She let me stay in my room for as long as I wanted, which was basically all night, except for the short break I took to grab a bowl of cereal. To Grams's credit, she never asked me any questions, only gave me a knowing smile that made me think that she somehow knew what was inside the box all along.

"Did you tell Grams about this?"

Quinn's eyes widen. "What?"

"About the box. About what you put inside of it."

Every news article inside the box had a headline more improbable, but also more amazing than the one I read before it. There was the one about the scientist in Greenland who claimed that by time-traveling she was able to add ten years on to her life, the one about the married couple from Japan who supposedly saved their dog by going back in time to fix the hole in their fence through which their dog had originally escaped, and there was the one where a preeminent professor at Massachusetts Institute of Technology was philosophizing about how not only did he believe that time travel was possible, but that he wouldn't be that surprised to hear that someone had already accomplished it. .

Every single article was short, though. They were glimpses, not fully fleshed-out studies. I knew I was going to need to do more research, but the moment I had that thought, I also knew that Quinn's idea had gotten inside of me in the way cold air slips in through a crack in a thin windowpane. I'd shivered and kept on reading.

"No." Quinn shakes her head. "I haven't told anyone. So that means you read the articles?"

"I don't know if you can really call them articles," I say, even though that's exactly what I've been calling them. "They're so short. They're more like summaries."

Quinn doesn't argue with me. She stays quiet. She's always been better at silence than me. I don't like silence at all. People need to be constantly talking or I get nervous. Quinn, though, she can ride it out. I've always envied that.

"So we need to do more research," I finally say, and I realize she's used silence again to her advantage. She's gotten me to show my hand. A tiny smile appears on her face.

"That is," I clarify, "if we work on this together. But I still don't know about it. It seems very theoretical."

"Isn't all science theoretical?"

I shrug. She's made a good point, but it's not like I'm going to admit that. "Plus, I shouldn't be talking to you."

"Because of what Parker did? Because he's the reason Mabel's dead?"

There's another whistle in the distance. I'm thankful for it because it helps distract me from the momentary shock of what Quinn just said. I can't believe she came out and, well, said it. Even Grams uses euphemisms when it comes to how Mabel died, saying things like *It was her time to pass* or *Now she's resting in peace*. When I told her that once, she told me that *euphemism* is a million-dollar word. I know Grams thinks it's snotty that I collect "million-dollar words," but I don't collect them to show off. I just like knowing things. The more things you know, the less likely you are to be taken by surprise.

I glance around. I wonder how many people have logged Quinn and me talking. They probably have decided I'm a rotten and traitorous sister. I don't blame them.

"Yes. Because of that," I say.

"But—" Quinn pauses. For a second, I worry that her brain is having one of its freeze-ups, but she gives me three blinks to signal that *no, she's not freezing up*, and *yes, she is fine*, and *she just needs a moment to collect her thoughts*.

"But?" I prompt.

"But we if we work together to change what happened, it's not really like you're . . ." Quinn shakes her head and tries again. "It's not like you're really hanging out with me or that you've forgiven me. It's because you want to help

49

Mabel. Sorry. I don't know if that makes sense." She bites the inside of her cheek. "I don't have the right words."

I frown. "Are you trying to say that it would be okay for us to hang out if we're working on this because it's not like I'm actually being your friend again, more that we're working together to . . ." It's my turn to grasp for words.

"Save Mabel," I finally settle on. The words tumble out of my mouth and land at my feet with the weight and pull of gravity. Dad is always reminding me that gravity is the most powerful force on the planet.

Quinn's tiny smile transforms into a lopsided grin. "I knew you would get it."

I tilt my head back. The sky is a shade of blue that I always see described in books as drinkable, but water actually isn't blue. It's clear. It's the sunlight that gives it color. And the sky only appears blue because of the length of the light rays coming from the sun. I used to tell Quinn facts like that all the time, but I'm going to keep this one to myself. I keep waiting for her to say something, to fill in the silence. She doesn't, of course. When I look at her, I find her patiently watching me.

I point at the direction of the athletic field. The team is dribbling balls around orange cones. "Does it bother you that you're not on the soccer team?"

"No. I'll play next year. Once I've fixed everything."

"You've?"

Her lopsided grin returns. "Okay. I mean we."

"I still don't know about this."

Her grin falters a little but doesn't disappear. "Can I show you something? It might help you make up your mind."

"Fine," I say, and it feels like opening another box.

EIGHT
QUINN

Dear Parker,

Cupcake misses you.

She purrs all the time, which confused me at first, because I didn't get how she could be so happy. Like I know she's a cat, so she probably doesn't really understand what happened, but I also think she does. Because cats know all things.

But then I remembered that Cora told me once that humans think cats purr because they're happy, but really cats purr for attention. It's their way of saying, "Hi, notice me," and, "I need a hug," and, "I want you around."

It's their way of saying, "Hey, don't leave me alone."

Why did you leave Cupcake alone? Why did you stop loving her?

I'll never forget the first day I saw that her food bowl was empty. I don't know how long it had been empty. I figured you just forgot.

But you didn't forget. I started feeding Cupcake after that.

Your sister,
Quinn

I lead Cora into the woods. She talks the entire time. I'd actually forgotten how much the girl can talk.

"Are you sure?" she says for the fifteenth time. "We're not supposed to walk through the forest preserve."

I hop over an exposed tree root and turn around to hold out my hand to help Cora. She surprises me by taking it.

"It'll be fine," I reassure her, also for the fifteenth time. "No one comes out here."

"Hikers do."

"So let's pretend to be hikers."

"But we're not hikers."

I let the argument drop after that. In exactly one second, she picks up again.

"So where are you taking me, anyway?"

I keep walking. Cora's footsteps are heavy behind me, crunching on stray twigs, so I know she's still following. The afternoon sunlight filters through the trees, making the floor of the forest turn a golden glowing brown. The air is crisp, a slight chill that wakes up your face.

"Come on, Quinn," Cora says. "This isn't funny."

"I wasn't telling a joke."

Her footsteps stop, so I turn around. She's standing there with her arms crossed. "You have to tell me where we're going."

"Your backpack looks like it weighs a million pounds," I say.

She pinches her lips together. Our preschool teacher called that particular expression a fish face. "If you're not careful, your face will get stuck like that, Miss Hamed," Mrs. Tanner would say. Cora got scared that her face actually would get stuck like that and Grams and I had to talk her down.

Cora's always taken things very literally. I mean, Mrs. Tanner would tell me that I was going to end up trapped in one of my daydreams if I didn't learn how to stay in the real world. I never freaked out about that.

Cora narrows her eyes. "What? I have a lot of homework."

"That makes sense. I mean, you're in Honors Math and Honors English, right?" This is the first year we've had tracked classes. I'm not in Honors anything.

Cora nods. "So where are we going?"

"I want to show this—" I'm not sure if my brain is actually having a Freeze-Up or if these things—or rather this thing—is just really tricky to talk about. Whenever I'm thinking really hard about time travel, my brain feels like a piece of butter that's going to slide right out of my skull and leak out onto the floor. Time travel is not an easy thing to understand and I don't want to look stupid in front of Cora.

Cora blinks at me. I blink back twice. My heart turns into a balloon every time she uses that signal with me, inflating with all my memories of Cora, inflating with all my love for her. *She doesn't think I'm stupid*, my brain says. *She still cares about me.* My heart inflates some more.

"I want to show you a place I think would be good to build our time machine," I say.

"I don't think we should build a time machine."

"What? You read the—"

"A time machine isn't practical."

I maneuver around under a low, spiky branch and make sure Cora does the same. The last thing I need is her getting a gnarly scratch before I've even had a chance to show her the giant oak tree. "You used to be fascinated with time machines."

"Yeah. When I was a kid."

My balloon of a heart deflates a little bit. "But all the articles—"

"They didn't say you had to have a time machine. Most of them mentioned wormholes."

"A time machine is a way to find a wormhole." I repeat

that fact with confidence. I've read it over and over again. I've whispered it to myself before falling asleep and whispered it again when I woke up in the morning.

"But not the only way. And there's no chance we could get the materials in time to build a machine. Wait. You weren't really suggesting that we build a time machine, were you? We would need like a gajillion dollars." Cora unfolds her fingers like she's counting.

I hadn't thought about that. I'd only imagined what the time machine would look like. A flashy dashboard with lots of fancy and futuristic knobs. A saucer shape with a metallic glow. Something beautiful, but also important-looking.

"I don't know," I say.

"Well, I don't think it's practical to build a time machine."

"Um. Okay." My brain is asking, *Then what?* But I don't say it.

"I think we should try to find a wormhole without a time machine," Cora answers my question without me having to ask.

"That's possible?"

"You read the articles, didn't you?"

I bite my lip. "Yes. I'm the one who found them."

"So then you should get what I'm saying."

This is starting to remind me of a reading comprehension test. Whenever I get a bad grade, I always try to explain

56

to Mom that I did read the book. And just because I can't remember what color shirt the character was wearing on page six doesn't mean that I didn't read it. I mean, I was too busy crying about the dead dog at the end to remember what the characters were wearing.

"You do, don't you?" Cora presses.

I nod my head yes even though I really don't get it, and I'm grateful that I'm still in front of Cora so she can't see my face. To me, a time machine equals time travel. We need a time machine. That seems like the most basic of basic things.

"We don't need a time machine if we can find a wormhole, right?" Cora says.

"Right," I parrot. "But how do we find a wormhole without a time machine?"

"That's the challenge!" Cora's voice is more animated than it's been all day. *Challenge* is a word that I've never been excited about. Challenges are puzzles and I'd almost forgotten how much Cora loves puzzles. Memories of sleepovers spent watching Cora put together a zillion pieces while I half-heartedly matched a few border pieces race through my head.

We reach the edge of the creek. I spot the giant oak tree on the other side. My heart cartwheels in my chest. This is my chance to show her that I'm not completely worthless. The giant oak tree is the zillion-piece puzzle that I've put together.

"Okay," I say, pointing at the creek. It rained some last

night, but the water still isn't very high. "We're gonna have to cross."

Cora's caught up with me by now. She's standing by my shoulder. She eyes the water and frowns. "I'm not sure about that."

"Come on, Core. It's not that big of a deal."

"Uh, I don't want to slip and fall."

"You won't. Here, watch me." I leap out onto the first rock and turn back to Cora. I stretch my hand out. "Come on. I won't let you slip."

Cora hesitates, but then she grabs my hand. We slowly cross to the other side of the bank this way, me hopping to the next rock, Cora reaching to grab on to me. She drops my hand once we're standing in front of the giant oak tree.

"This is it," I say, my voice small and quiet like its three inches tall, a mushroom of a voice.

She cranes her head back to look all the way up at the tree. "This is what you wanted to show me?"

"I think—" I start, and then correct myself. "I feel like there's a wormhole here. I call it the giant oak tree."

"The giant oak tree," Cora repeats.

I study the tree again. *Please see what I see.* Its trunk—wide and expansive, its armlike branches stretching out in every direction, and the bulge of bark that looks like an eyeball. "Do you see that?" I point. "It's like an eye."

"Yeah," Cora says. "I see that."

I hold my breath, the tiniest bit of hope bubbling up inside of me.

"What makes you think there's a wormhole here?"

"I don't know. I mean, I feel it."

Cora wrinkles her nose. "You feel it?"

I should've known she wouldn't like that answer. "I mean," I correct, "from everything I've read, it matches the description."

"What description?"

"You know. Of places that have wormholes."

She walks closer to the tree. "Hm. I guess I see what you're saying."

"You do?"

Cora bends over to inspect the tree, running her fingers over the moss on the bark. I hope she doesn't see that as a negative. I thought it was a good thing that the tree was able to be a home for other living things. That it was able to grow things.

"Yeah. So now we just need a plan for how to make the wormhole appear." She turns to me, and there's a smile on her face.

It's the first time I've seen her smile all day.

It's the first time I've seen her smile since November 11 last year.

"A plan. You've always been good at those."

She nods, her hazel eyes bright and wide. "I have some ideas already. I think we should probably structure all of this like a science experiment. Does that make sense to you?"

She doesn't wait for me to respond; she keeps talking, "So we'll have a hypothesis and then different steps. Coming up with the hypothesis should be easy, but I want to take some time to make sure we get it right. Also, it seems like there are conflicting ideas about how to make wormholes appear. Did you pick up on that, too, when you read the articles? Some of them implied that wormholes—"

Cora keeps talking about the different theories surrounding wormholes. I know I should pay attention, but I find my mind drifting.

Time travel. Wormholes. Fabric of the universe.

I imagine a door appearing in the middle of the giant oak tree's trunk. A magic door, a door that glows with light. It will be covered with moss and have a big brass handle. We'll open it, and *whoosh.*

There's my brother. I squeeze my eyes shut. I'm not sure how to envision this next part. Do I want to see him on that terrible morning? I never actually saw him on that day—I only heard his boots in the hallway.

But I don't think I want to see him then. I want to see him before. But when? My heart skids like a car zooming over ice as I shift through memories. Doors being slammed. The time he grabbed my wrist. The hateful comments he made. The back of his head as he walked toward Dad's safe. I let out a tiny yelp.

"Quinn?" Cora says. "Are you listening?"

I startle. "Huh? Oh yeah. I agree with everything you're saying."

Cora wrinkles her nose again. Overhead, a group of birds are flying in a triangular pattern, a dark splotch against the blue sky. The noise of their flapping wings fills the woods; it sounds like rain pattering against a roof.

"Is there"—I rack my brain for the right word—"a scientific term for a group of birds?" This is the type of question Cora always knows the answer to.

"Flock," Cora responds quickly. "Well, usually. But some subspecies of birds have more specific names for a group of them. Like a group of falcons is called a 'bazaar.'"

"'Bazaar,'" I repeat.

"Did you know that human ears are trained to hear the chirping of birds?" Cora asks even though I know she doesn't expect me to answer. "I heard that once on one of the podcasts Dad listens to."

"Of all the sounds in the world," she continues, "we hear birds best of all. And you know why that is? You'd think it might be the roar of lions or the sound of some other predator, right? But no. We hear the chirps of birds because where there are birds, there usually is water. And where there is water, there's life. We're biologically programmed to favor life. Not fear. Isn't that so cool?"

"So cool," I whisper, looking up at the birds. They're almost out of view now, near the edge of the sky, their flapping a distant hum.

I didn't realize how much I've missed this part of Cora until now. Her mind is like a treasure chest of mind-blowing facts. And when she shares them with you, it makes you start to believe that the world is actually a pretty amazing place. It makes you see everything a little differently.

I'm trying to figure out how to tell her this, when I see that her eyes are glossy. She hunches over, grasping her backpack straps. She makes a sucking sound with her mouth.

I know that sound.

It's the vacuuming of tears, the desperate suctioning-up of salt and sadness. When you do it, you feel like you're choking. When you do it, it's because you feel like you have no other choice.

"Core," I say. "It's—"

She holds up her hand. Another sucking sound. This time louder. She wipes snot away from her nose. "I'm sorry. I thought I could do this, but I can't. This is insane." She gestures toward the giant oak tree. "I just can't."

She takes off into the woods. I shout after her, but she doesn't turn around.

I'm left. Alone.

The sky's empty. There's not a bird in sight.

NINE
CORA

I reach for the buzzer, but I'm too slow. Peter Tolbin, an eighth grader who smells strongly of leather-scented Axe body spray, beats me to it once again.

"The naked mole rat," he says.

"Correct," Coach Pearlman says, and awards a point to the eighth graders. I find it annoying that when we scrimmage, we are always divided into seventh versus eighth grade. First, we're one team. Second, the eighth grade has a major advantage—they've been on Quiz Bowl for a whole year longer than us. But I know Coach Pearlman wouldn't appreciate me complaining, so I keep my mouth shut and stare sourly at the bald eagle poster hanging in the corner of Coach's classroom. The bald eagle is flying across a bright blue sky and there's white script underneath it that says *Soar with Attitude*. It's the only decoration Coach Pearlman has up. He's what Grams would call a "minimalist."

"I thought that was your category," Mia whispers to me.
"Naked mole rats?"

She laughs a little, and Coach Pearlman casts us a warning look. "Not specifically, but you know."

She's right. I'm usually pretty good at the Nature and Wildlife category because Dad always listens to all these biology podcasts in the car. So I've grown up around facts like cows kill more people a year than sharks and the average snake sheds its skin four times per year, but when they are babies, they shed their skin every two weeks.

But honestly? I don't have a favorite category. Math, spelling, history—I'm pretty good at them all. Well, usually. Today though I don't seem to be capable of recalling any facts that don't have to do with wormholes.

Even though I ran off on Quinn, I can't stop thinking about the idea of time travel. I stayed up late last night rereading all the articles that were in the box and googling tips for making wormholes appear. I know it is all probably nonsense, but I can't stop looking things up.

A loud timer goes off. Coach Pearlman stands up and clears his throat. "Okay, that's round one. So far, we've got eighth grade with eleven points and seventh grade with three points."

Mia, Owen, and I all exchange a frown.

"But take heart, I have a feeling you may do well with

the next category. Middle Eastern Geography," Coach Pearlman says and looks right at the seventh-grade side of the room.

Owen and I exchange a glance. We both make faces, and I'm not sure whether I feel like laughing or crying. Owen and I talk about this a lot. Like how uncomfortable it is that teachers ask him strangely personal questions about the economy in Japan, and the people who assume I know everything about the war in Iraq just because my dad is from Lebanon, which I guess is vaguely in the same region but definitely not the same thing. I've always been a little jealous of Owen because he does at least know some things about Japan. His parents took him one summer to visit his grandparents in Kyoto. I've never been to Lebanon, and Dad hardly ever talks about it.

I've also seen people confuse Owen as being Chinese and have witnessed classmates ask him if he's related to Ben Park, who is in our grade and is Korean. Sometimes people ask me if I'm Mexican or Indian. It's just hard to constantly feel like your identity is up for debate or that it's okay for strangers to make random guesses about it. Owen understands how strange and bad that can feel. No one ever asks Mia where she's from.

"Is Coach P. talking to you?" Mia whispers at Owen. "Japan isn't even in the Middle East. That's ridiculous."

"He probably meant Cora. But it's ridiculous either

way." Owen flashes me a broad smile. I know he's annoyed, too, but he's better than me at hiding it.

Mia looks incredulous. That's a million-dollar word I learned in preparation for Quiz Bowl. "Cora?" she says, her mouth pinching into an O shape.

Owen glances at me, his goofy smile morphing into something more awkward. "Her dad."

"Oh. That's right," Mia says.

I can't decide if it's worse when people totally forget about that part of my identity or when people make assumptions about it. Both of them feel like losing. I hate losing.

The questions start. "The capital of Saudi Arabia is—"

Mia reaches for the buzzer. She looks over at me. I give her a blank look. The timer beeps.

"Eighth grade's turn," Coach Pearlman announces.

"Riyadh," Molly Waldheim answers confidently. Molly is an eighth grader and my Quiz Bowl idol. She's the singular reason our school's team made it to state last year. She wears these shiny silver barrettes in her hair. I really want to buy a pair for myself, but I don't want it to seem like I'm copying her.

Mabel would be able to tell me whether it would be too geeky slash too creepy for me to get the same ones as her. My older sister knew about things like that. She's the one who taught me to look right at the space between someone's eyebrows if you're too nervous to look them in the eye.

When Mabel was still alive, I kept a running list of things to ask her. These days, I still have questions, but I don't have anyone to ask.

"Correct." Coach Pearlman gives Molly a thumbs-up and awards the eighth graders another point.

I might be imagining it, but I swear he also gives me a look. My cheeks burn. I know that it's silly that Coach Pearlman thinks I should know more about the Middle East than anyone else, but also, I feel like I should.

The round continues. We get a couple of questions right but end up losing pretty badly. "Okay. I've got one more section of practice questions planned, but let's take a short break. Regroup in five minutes," Coach Pearlman announces before heading to his desk to pull out his supposedly secret stash of snacks that we all actually know about. He not so discreetly shoves a handful of pretzels into his mouth.

Mia rests her weight on her elbows. "You sure you're okay?"

"You keep asking me that."

She grimaces like she's offended. "Well, you keep acting—"

"Acting like what? Because I didn't know the answers to the capitals of those countries? My dad's from Lebanon, not Saudi Arabia—in case you forgot," I say, raising my voice.

"I know. I'm not talking about that. You don't have to yell at me."

I cross my arms. "I'm not yelling at you."

"Hey," Owen interjects. "Quick question. Do you trust self-driving cars?"

"Definitely," Mia says. "Robots are more reliable than humans."

"Humans are the ones that will build the robots, though. They'll only be as reliable as their code. So I don't know," I say. "Though theoretically speaking, you could say all of us are simply made up of codes."

"Solid points." Owen nods, his dark brown eyes warm as he considers what we're saying. My stomach goes all fizzy again, but this time I'm not that mad about it. It feels so much better than arguing with Mia did.

"Chances of extraterrestrial life?" I say, smiling at Owen.

"Astronomically high!" he answers.

"I agree," Mia says.

"That's boring. You two are supposed to have different opinions," I say.

"Sorry to disappoint, but you're not going to get me to argue against the possibility of aliens," Mia says.

"Science is pretty clear on the issue," Owen agrees.

I see the opening. This is my chance to get their take on wormholes. At the very least, I can find out if they believe in them. But right when I'm about to ask, Coach Pearlman calls us back to attention to start round three of the scrimmage.

So I try to stop thinking about wormholes, and instead focus on getting some points. My hand hovers over the buzzer.

After all, answers are always better than questions.

TEN

QUINN

Dear Parker,

The first time you called Cora's dad "a nasty foreigner," I froze.

I wanted to think you were kidding. But you weren't kidding. You even called me a "stupid female" and you kept saying stuff like that over and over again. I never said anything back. I wish I had. I should've.

Mom did a couple of times. But then she gave up. I think Dad pretended like he didn't hear you. I once heard him tell Mom that you were going through "a phase."

I'm so mad at you, Parker. Sometimes I even hate you. But it's so scary to hate you.

And I hate being scared all the time.

Your sister,
Quinn

When Mom found out that Dad was going to be home for dinner, she completely changed the meal plan.

"I'm sure Dad would be happy to eat anything," I'd told her, but she'd insisted on cooking something more special.

"It's not every day we get to have a real family dinner," she'd said, pulling out a bag of leafy greens, eggs, and raw beef. She announced her plan to make homemade meatballs and pasta and a fresh salad, and I stopped arguing then because it all sounded delicious.

But now that Dad is here, I'm realizing that it doesn't matter what is on the menu because it's hard to have an appetite once the fighting starts. Usually Mom and Dad save their arguments for when they think I'm asleep and can't hear them, but tonight it's clear that they don't care that I'm sitting right in front of their faces.

"So I drove by something interesting today," Dad says, forking at one of the meatballs. He chews with one side of his mouth and talks out the other. "A beautiful house in Turner's Point."

Mom takes a long drink of water and gulps loudly. That swallow is a warning sign, a blinking yellow light, proceed with caution. "I thought you had a busy day. How did you have time to drive all the way out to Turner's Point?"

Dad sets down his fork. He pulls at his tie, loosening it a little. "Come on, Clarissa. Turner's Point isn't that far from us. And it's definitely not that far from my office. My commute would be about the same."

Mom's face goes stony. "Daniel, let's not talk about this. Especially not in front of Quinn." She gives me the world's sourest smile—it's all lemons.

It's Dad's turn for a loud swallow. I want to crawl under the table. I glance around for Cupcake, but she's nowhere to be found. She's probably hiding upstairs. Smart cat.

"Well"—Dad's eyes shift to me—"I was thinking I'd like to get Quinn's take on this."

I know from those late-night conversations that I'm not supposed to hear that Dad has been wanting to move for a long time. He says that we all need a fresh start. He also wants to buy a less expensive house because apparently money things aren't great between Mom leaving her job and the legal fees surrounding what happened with Parker.

Mom doesn't give me the chance to answer. She sets her water glass down with a bang. "We aren't moving. Chestnut is our home."

"Q, honey," Dad says. "Are things . . ." He stops talking. He looks off in the distance. When Dad was younger, his brain also used to Freeze Up. Maybe that's what's happening right now.

He shakes his head a little and starts again. "Are things hard for you? Would you like a fresh start? A chance to make new friends?"

At this, Mom stands up. She snatches the serving plate of pasta and walks over to the sink. She dumps it all into the trash, which is a real bummer because I was hoping to eat more later when the fighting stopped and I could stomach it.

"Uh," I say. There are so many things I want to say, but so many things I know that I can't.

"You can be honest with us, Q," Dad says. He tilts forward in his chair, and I push back in mine.

"How dare you, Daniel!" Mom's voice is high and strained. My shoulders lurch toward my ears as I sink down in my seat. "You can't ask her questions like that. We're raising her to be strong and resilient. Not to run away from her problems."

"Resilient," Dad says. "Right. That's another one of your parenting buzzwords. Look how well that worked out with—"

Mom spins around. She wags a finger at him, and I see her short and ragged her fingernail is. It's clear she's been biting them. "They were yours. Remember that. They were yours."

They were yours. My heart experiences a tiny earthquake, a shake and shudder. She's talking about the guns. Dad's guns. The guns that Parker used.

Dad shakes his head again. More firmly this time. He

73

stands up and shoves his chair back into the table, its legs screeching against the floor. "How many times are we going to have this fight, Clarissa? I was responsible. They were legally purchased. And . . ." He pinches the bridge of his nose. "What does it matter? They're gone now."

"That's right. You were *responsible*," Mom says.

"They're gone now," Dad repeats, hanging his head.

"And so is my son," Mom says. Her face isn't stony anymore. It's melting—all tears and snot. "I'm not losing my home, too. Do you get that, Daniel? I'm not losing this house. This is our home."

She leans back against the kitchen counter. Her shoulders tremble as her crying gets louder.

I want so badly to hug her, but I can't bring myself to move.

Dad squeezes Mom's shoulder, but she pushes him away. Before he leaves the room, he gives me a look that I don't understand. I wish I did.

Even once Dad's gone, Mom keeps crying. I can feel the jab of tears in my own eyes, but I'm not allowed to cry. I squeeze my eyes shut and picture the giant oak tree. I see its long muscled armlike branches and thick trunk with the bumpy bark. I imagine the wormhole opening up right in the center of it. A glowing door. I imagine it so hard that I think my brain might burst.

"I'm going to make things better," I whisper. Mom doesn't hear me, but I really hope the universe does.

ELEVEN

CORA

Grams waves the car keys in the air. "Come on, baby girl. We've got to get going. Your dad's going to meet us there."

Dad rearranged his whole class schedule so that he can always make my Dr. Randall appointments. I told him that wasn't necessary—it's not like Grams or him even go into the appointment with me—they just sit in the hall and wait for the session to be over. Sometimes they catch up with Dr. Randall after, but usually they just wave to him and we go on our way. I'd be lying though if I said knowing that Dad was sitting in the hallway wasn't comforting to me. It feels nice to know for that forty-five minutes exactly where Grams and he are. Ever since Mabel died, I've spent a lot of time calculating the whereabouts of people I love. I've learned that no one is ever really safe, even when it seems like they should be.

That might actually be the worst thing I've learned, and I've learned a lot of terrible things.

Grams is mostly quiet on the drive, but I can tell she wants to ask me about the box. She's doing her off-beat humming thing she does whenever she's trying to stop herself from talking.

"I opened it," I say with a sigh. "But you know that."

She stops at a red light and looks at me in the rearview mirror. "I didn't say anything."

"You might as well have," I mumble.

"Did you talk to her?"

"Yeah, but it's not like we're friends again."

"It wouldn't be so bad if you were."

"Yes, it would be."

Grams lets out a whistle-like sound. "Let's agree to disagree, sweet pea."

"I hate that phrase."

"I know you do. Regardless, I'm proud of you, Cora London."

"It was only a box."

Grams gives me a small smile at the next red light. "Well, still."

She off-beat hums the rest of the drive. I don't say anything else, though.

Dr. Randall's office is in a strip mall, sandwiched between a Chinese restaurant and a hair salon. Lots of times after my appointments, Grams, Dad, and I go to the Chinese place and order a huge plate of noodles and a tray of egg rolls. Depending on how sorry he's feeling for me, Dad sometimes even lets me get a soda. He never used to let me get sodas, but that's one of the few perks of having a dead sister—I'm now allowed to drink Coke.

"Hello, Cora," Dr. Randall greets me in the hallway of his office and motions for me to come into the room. I give Grams a small wave and follow after Dr. Randall.

I sit on the comfy leather couch across from his large arm chair. Dr. Randall is Black with dark skin and graying hair. He wears oval-shaped glasses and likes to make a "mmm" sound with his lips whenever I say something that he finds interesting. Which seems to be about just everything I say. That's one nice thing about my visits with Dr. Randall—he makes me feel like every thought I have is important.

"So how are you feeling this week, Cora?"

"I don't know."

He makes that "mmm" sound. "I looked at the calendar today. The anniversary is coming up."

My stomach clenches. I don't want to think about the anniversary. "It's only September."

Dr. Randall nods in agreement. "But soon it will be October. And then it will be November 11."

That's another thing I like about Dr. Randall—he just comes out and says things. Lots of adults in my town can barely say that date aloud, but Dr. Randall is different. He says the hard things in the exact same way he says the easy things, which makes me think that someday I'm going to be able to do that, too.

Today is not that day, though. I squirm on the couch, crossing and then uncrossing my ankles. My eyes focus on Dr. Randall's framed diploma from Howard University. Next they settle on a carved wooden statue that's on his desk. I've asked him about it before. It was a gift from his wife. There's a framed Basquiat print on the wall and a thick art book on the center table. Dr. Randall's wife is an artist. I'm looking for anything that we can talk about except the thing that we're talking about, but there isn't anything in this room that I haven't asked him about a zillion times before.

"It understandably is going to bring up a lot of different emotions for you. Would you like to talk about that?"

I look over at the essential oil diffuser. It's gurgling up bursts of lavender and eucalyptus. Dr. Randall doesn't rush me to answer. He never does.

When I first started coming here, I didn't really want to talk to Dr. Randall. But I also don't know how to sit and be quiet for an hour, so I ended up chatting his ears off. To my surprise, Dr. Randall actually has some pretty solid advice.

"I don't know," I finally say. "I don't like the idea of the anniversary. It's like it will somehow make it more real."

Dr. Randall adjusts his glasses. "That's very valid, Cora. Anniversaries are often fraught with emotion for that reason. It can be nice to commemorate the event, as there is power in remembrance, but it can also be very difficult to have to almost relive your trauma from that day."

Fraught. That's a good word. I make a mental note to remember it in case it comes up in a Quiz Bowl question. It's another one of those words that sounds like what it means. Those are my favorite.

"I talked to Quinn," I blurt out. Dr. Randall knows all about Quinn. I've talked about her a lot.

Dr. Randall's expression stays calm, but he leans toward me with interest. "Really? How did that come about?"

"She left me a box. As a birthday present."

"Oh. I suppose that's nice of her. What was the present?"

I hesitate. I tell Dr. Randall lots of things, but I don't think I can tell him about what was in the box. "That's not important."

"Okay," he says, his voice level. "What would you like to share about your conversation?"

I cross my arms. I wish I could fold myself up like a pretzel. "Nothing really."

"Are you sure?"

"I told her that I can't be her friend."

Dr. Randall makes the "mmm" sound with his lips again. "You still feel that way, huh?"

"I can't be friends with the person who is responsible for my sister's death."

"Well, as we've talked about before, Quinn isn't truly responsible, is she?"

I shake my head. My throat has a tight burning feeling. It's a pre-crying feeling I'm all too familiar with. I try to gulp down my tears, but it's no use. The pressure builds behind my eyes and slowly, but surely, I feel the tears glide down my cheeks. "You know what I'm trying to say, though."

"I do," Dr. Randall confirms. "But I still think it's important to make that distinction."

Another thing I like about Dr. Randall: he doesn't react when I cry. Not in a mean way, but in a way that makes me feel like it's okay to cry. He doesn't make a big deal about it.

"You know, Cora," Dr. Randall says, "it's okay for you to feel confused about how you feel about Quinn. It's okay for you to miss your friend and feel guilty about it. We can talk about those things in here. This is a safe space for you to talk about all your emotions. There's no judgment here."

I shake my head again. My eyes are blurry with tears. "You always say that this is a safe space."

"Because it is," Dr. Randall says.

"But how can you say that? How do you know? Because you know what I know? I know that any space can be safe until it isn't anymore." My voice cracks a little.

I stare down at my shoes. They're my black sneakers that Mabel never approved of. I wear these sneakers all the time now because when I wear them, I can hear her teasing me about them. Sometimes at night I try on her shoes. Her strappy sandals and leather ballet flats. The shoes she never would've let me borrow if she were still alive.

"You know what? You're right, Cora. I meant that this is a safe space for you to explore your emotions. But I understand given the trauma you've experienced how it will be difficult for you to view any place as a safe space," Dr. Randall says.

I look up at him. He meets my gaze. "Do you understand what I'm saying, Cora?"

I don't really, but it seems rude not to nod. I'm not used to admitting that I don't understand things.

He taps his fingers slowly against the arm of his leather chair. "It's okay for you to not feel okay. You know that, right?"

My throat is still tight. "It doesn't feel like it is."

"Well, it is."

"I just want to be okay. I don't want to *feel* okay. I want to *be* okay."

He gives me a soft smile. "I know. And guess what? Allowing yourself to be not okay sometimes is that big first step to actually being okay." His smile widens. "Being okay with not being okay is a very important and difficult emotional maturity to reach. Lots of adults don't even have it."

Right then, he looks up at the clock. Our session is over. He stands up and I do the same. "I'll see you next week."

Grams and Dad are waiting for me in the hallway. They stand on either side of me, each one draping an arm around my shoulder. For the shortest of moments, I feel safe. Like I still live in a world where I can believe that nothing bad happens.

"Dinner?" Dad asks.

I nod and discreetly try to wipe away the leftover tears from my eyes. Dad, unlike Dr. Randall, takes my tears personally.

We walk next door to the Chinese restaurant. We sit at our usual table by the window. Dad lets me get a large soda. I fill it up to the top with Coke.

"How was your session?" Dad asks as he forks a large portion of lo mein onto his plate.

"Saeed," Grams says gently. "You know Cora doesn't have to tell us that."

It's funny to me how Grams parents my dad even though he isn't her son. In lots of way the whole situation is a little different, how she stayed with us even after Mom left. I asked her about it once and she waved me off saying that she was lucky that Dad let her stick around. It's harder to ask Dad about it because he gets really awkward whenever I bring up Mom. Once, though, he told me that in a way being an immigrant feels a lot like being an orphan, and with that logic, Grams is his American mother and he'll always feel grateful for that.

Dad's parents died when he was young. He was raised by his aunt in Lebanon. She died when I was only four. I don't know much about the rest of the family. Dad doesn't talk about them much, and I'm worried that if I ask questions, I'll only make him sad. Occasionally, he'll say something about this cousin or that cousin, and I store the information. I keep hoping that if I collect enough facts, I'll be able to complete the puzzle.

"I know," Dad says, chewing through a mouthful of noodles. Dad might be an esteemed professor of molecular biology, but he still talks with his mouth full. "I was just seeing if she wanted to share anything."

"It was okay," I say, splitting an egg roll in half.

Dad wiggles his eyebrows. "Okay. The most descriptive word in the English language."

I take another large sip of my Coke. "Do your first years use that word a lot?"

Dad laughs. "I haven't heard it too much yet, and it'll hopefully stay that way, *inshallah*." Dad usually doesn't teach first years—he actually hardly ever teaches undergraduates, but this semester he's teaching a Bio 101 class because the university president asked him to. The president said it would be good publicity for the university, but all the broken glassware and lab reports filled with typos are driving Dad nuts.

"You need to be nicer on those kids," Grams says, and

she squeezes Dad's arm affectionately. "Remember that once upon a time you were just starting out, too."

Dad grumbles and stares down at his plate of noodles. Something crosses over his face and I wonder if he's thinking about his time in college, which means he's probably thinking about Mom.

"Does Mom know about Mabel?" I don't realize I've actually asked that question aloud until I see Dad's and Grams's faces.

Gram balls up a napkin in her hand and Dad keeps staring at his noodles. The only other customer in the restaurant is a young guy with a baseball cap who is eating a big plate of food all by himself, so the whole room goes quiet enough that I can hear the clanking of dishes in the restaurant's kitchen.

"Corrie, honey," Grams says slowly, looking over at Dad.

Dad shakes his head a little. "The honest answer is I'm not sure, Cora. I didn't hear from her. I would guess she's aware if she follows the news."

"It didn't get a lot of news coverage." This is something me and every other person in Chestnut is pretty bitter about. Not that I wanted reporters following me around for months, shoving a microphone in my face. It hurt, though, in a way I didn't expect, that reporters swarmed our town the day it happened, but then left the day after when it was clear the body count wasn't high enough to merit front-page coverage.

My sister was dead and that wasn't even remarkable enough to be national news for longer than approximately five minutes.

"If she's paying attention, she knows," Grams says.

"That's what I'm asking." I scrape my fork across my plate. "Is she paying attention?"

"Corrie," Grams says, and she reaches across the table to hold my hand. I let her even though it makes me feel like a baby. "Where is this coming from? Is this what you talked about in your session?"

"I thought we weren't supposed to ask her about her session," Dad mumbles, a little bit of a teasing tone in his voice. I can tell he's trying to lighten the mood.

I know I should stop talking. Talking about Mom is always trouble.

"I just want to know that she misses Mabel. That she's sad about what happened to Mabel." I stare at both of their faces. "Don't you think she should be? Mabel's mom should miss her. Mabel deserves that." It's only when I see a tear-drop on my plate that I realize I'm crying again.

"Honeybee," Grams says, and she squeezes my hand tight. "Mabel is missed. She's missed by me and your dad and, most of all, she's missed by you. That's more than enough."

Dad's lips move, but he doesn't say anything. I catch Grams giving Dad one of her sideways looks.

"Grams is right," he says slowly. "But more importantly, she's loved by so many people. The love is even bigger than the missing."

I guess he's right, but sometimes the missing feels so big in my heart that I forget what the love even felt like.

TWELVE
QUINN

Dear Parker,

Occasionally when I picture the wormhole appearing,
I imagine it looking a lot like your bedroom door. You
had that sign that said "Do Not Open" in big ugly
letters.

I should've opened it.

I'm trying to open it now.

I hope it isn't too late.

Your sister,
Quinn

When the alarm sounds, I'm in art class, sketching a pumpkin on the black butcher paper that Mrs. Euclid has draped
across the long library tables. Our project this month is

making decorations for the fall festival.

Mrs. Euclid is the school librarian and the art teacher. I think it's pretty cool that she's able to wear two hats like that, but other people complain that it's because our school doesn't have the money to afford a real art teacher.

But Mrs. Euclid is real enough for me.

"Okay. You all know what to do," Mrs. Euclid says as the loud wail of the siren fills up the room. I try to curb the panic building inside of me by reminding myself it's only a drill, but it doesn't work.

We slide out of our chairs and head to the middle row of shelves. It's the place in the library that's the farthest from any doors or windows. We clump together. Those of us in the back of the clump have our spines pressed against the spines of books. The kids in front of us press their backs into our knees. Some kids whisper while Mrs. Euclid is away, securing the room. I stay quiet. Like we're supposed to. I'm not someone who can afford to break the rules.

Ainsley and Scarlett are sitting in front of me. I stare at the back of their soccer jerseys. Wednesdays are always terrible, even without a lockdown drill, because that's the day that the girls' soccer team has games, and they all wear their jerseys to school. If it's an away game, the jersey is pearl white with a navy lion emblazoned on the front. Today their jerseys are navy, which means it's a home game.

A 10 is written in big block numbers on the back of Ainsley's jersey. It feels like touching a hot stove when I look at it. Ten was always my number.

"You don't have to be so scared, Quinn," Scarlett says. She turns her head to look at me. Her white skin is slightly flushed and her blond hair is in two perfect French braids with navy bows at the ends. Scarlett's mom used to do our hair before games when we played rec league together. Once she put my hair in a waterfall braid and I scored three goals. That was a good day.

"This is just a drill. Your brother is gone, so . . ." Scarlett doesn't say anything else but pinches her lips together to give me a pointed look that says everything.

"Scarlett," Ainsley says in a warning tone, and there's a blush creeping up her light brown cheeks. Ainsley is biracial. Her dad is Indian and her mom is white. Her brown eyes gaze at me sympathetically as she plays with a loose strand of her black hair. I can tell she wants to tell me to ignore Scarlett, but isn't willing to say that out loud.

Scarlett's always had a mean streak. It's just, up until last year, it was never directed at me. Now I'm starting to feel bad about all the girls that I didn't stand up for, like when Scarlett used to tease Marissa for being a slow runner or Jackie for sweating so much that her uniform had pit stains.

Mrs. Euclid doesn't hear Scarlett because she's too busy shoving a desk against the door. That's her job during these drills, to find the heaviest object and use it to block the entrance to the library.

Thankfully Scarlett leaves me alone after that one

comment. But what she said didn't even bother me that much. I say worse things to myself all the time.

Scarlett goes back to talking with Ainsley about the game. Other kids in my class talk about their math homework and the fall festival and no one seems scared at all. When Mrs. Euclid comes back, they all go quiet again. No one is supposed to talk during these drills. The idea is that you don't want someone to be able to find you.

I'm holding my breath, but I'm not exactly scared.

I'm scared because I'm not scared. Because I know that if someone like Parker wanted to come hurt us all, he could. And he would.

This isn't the way to stop him.

I squeeze my eyes shut and picture the giant oak tree and the wormhole that I know is there, the wormhole I just need to make appear.

The alarm stops. I open my eyes, and for a brief moment, I swear there's a halo of light on the floor of the library.

A wormhole.

My heart leaps. I stand up so quickly that I bump my head on the edge of the bookshelf.

"Quinn!" Mrs. Euclid says. "Are you okay?"

I rub my head. When I look back at that spot on the carpet, the halo of light is gone. Disappointment wells up inside of me.

Mrs. Euclid struggles to move back the desk she'd shoved

against the door. My classmates return to their seats. They keep talking about soccer games and the fall festival and math quizzes. But I can't stop staring at the carpet.

It was there. I know it was there.

"Are you okay?" Mrs. Euclid sits down next to me. She points at my pumpkin. "That's some impressive shading. I like the dimension on that."

I stare down at the pumpkin I've drawn. It does look pretty good. It looks real. I've taken an image from my brain and brought it to life.

That's never happened before. My mind whirls. I think of the light on the carpet. I think of the door appearing in the trunk of the giant oak tree. I think about fixing everything.

THIRTEEN
CORA

It takes me a moment to realize everyone else is getting out of their seats. The alarm is ringing, but the only thing I hear is my own heartbeat.

My lungs ache like they're underwater. I'm gulping for air. I picture Mabel on that morning, on November 11. Did she think it was just a drill? Did they even have a lockdown?

I don't know the answer to that. Whenever I try to imagine my sister's last moments, my brain shuts down like a computer rebooting. It can't go there.

"Cora," Owen says, his voice half of a whisper. "Come on." He motions to the supply closet where the rest of our class is headed. I know I should move, but I can't. My legs are like lead.

Mrs. Darling, our English teacher, comes over to stand beside me. Mrs. Darling is white and has curly orange hair. Her long skirt swooshes against the classroom's floor. It is a soothing sound. That swoosh. I focus on that.

She bends down to whisper in my ear. "It's only a drill, Cora. It's okay."

I stiffly nod, but I still don't move. I don't even open my eyes.

"Can you please take a seat in the closet? It's protocol."

The classroom has gone quiet. There's no more whispering. When I open my eyes, I realize everyone is staring at me.

The stinging terror doesn't completely go away, but it's joined by a chilly humiliation. The books we read for English class describe shame as feeling hot, but for me, it's a cold emotion. Hollow and isolating.

I slide out of my chair and walk to the supply closet with Owen. Once we get there, I take a seat on the ground and hug my knees to my chest.

"These things are awful," he says quietly. "Are you okay?"

I don't say anything.

"Please don't worry. Mrs. Darling said it's only a drill," Owen says.

"Did you know that as humans domesticated and bred cows for slaughter that they evolved to have smaller brains?"

"Cora," Owen says. I know he wants me to stop talking. We're supposed to be silent during drills. Everyone is still staring at me.

"They developed smaller brains because it was better for

them not to understand. Do you get what I'm saying?"

"Cora," he says again. "Come on. It's only a drill, okay?"

Hot tears prick at my eyes. "But it's not always a drill. Sometimes it's real."

FOURTEEN
QUINN

Dear Parker,

Do you remember that summer at Gammie and Papa's house? You were so patient with me. I was scared of the roar of the waves and I would run whenever the water rushed up on the sand and tickled my toes. But you held my hand and stayed with me. You showed me how not to be scared of the water. You taught me to be brave.

I'm trying to find my way back to the Parker from that summer.

I'm trying to be brave like that again.

Your sister,
Quinn

I don't like opening the door to Parker's room. It's like somehow turning the knob lets out a ghost. But I also can't stay away.

Parker's room is mostly the same. His bed and shelf with dusty Little League trophies. The walls are painted a boring beige color. When he was little, his room was a bright orange. I don't remember when it changed color.

His computer is missing because the police took it. I don't know if they ever gave it back, but Mom didn't bother to set it up again. She also took down his corkboard. Both Parker and I have always had a corkboard. I don't know what was on his when he died. I don't think I want to know.

I flop on the top of his bed and stare up at the smooth white ceiling of his room. Cupcake joins me, sitting right on my chest and purring so loud that I can hardly hear myself think. But that's okay. I don't really want to think when I'm in my brother's room.

Because I know it's in this room that he decided to become the type of person who did the horrible thing that he did. It's in this room that he decided to become full of hate. I glance all around, looking for clues to what led him to it, but I don't find any.

There's a knock on the door, and I startle. I expect to see Mom's face, but it's Dad who is standing in the doorway.

He doesn't come in. Maybe he's also afraid of the ghosts.

"You okay, Q?"

Grown-ups love to ask that question. I'm starting to think they ask it more because they aren't okay themselves, but they don't know how to tell you that, so they want you to say it for them.

"Sure," I say. I scratch the space between Cupcake's ears.

"I'm home from work early."

That's another thing grown-ups, especially my dad, do a lot. State the obvious.

He scratches the back of his head. "Want to kick the ball around?"

He's still dressed in his work clothes. Slacks, button-down shirt, and a tie. We haven't kicked the ball around since last November.

"Um," I say. My brain is doing a major Freeze-Up.

"I mean," he says, raising up his hands, "it's fine if you don't want to. I just thought it might be fun."

I swallow multiple times. "Okay," I manage.

He gives me a tight smile. "Meet you downstairs in five?"

The air outside is chilly. I wear my old soccer sweatshirt. It's not nearly as cool as the one I would've gotten if I was actually on the seventh-grade team, but I've kept it because it reminds me that, once upon a time, I did actually belong to a team. Even if it was a rec league one.

Dad has already gotten the ball out of the garage. He's standing awkwardly in our backyard that's filled with

97

overgrown weedy grass. Dad used to mow the lawn every weekend, but he hasn't seemed to care about that in a while. He kicks the ball to me, and I trap it between my feet with ease.

I smile a little. I've still got it. I kick the ball back to Dad. We pass it back and forth for a while in silence.

"So how was school?" Dad says.

I kick the ball with a little more oomph. "We had a drill."

Dad doesn't manage to trap it. He runs to catch up with it. "A drill?"

"For lockdown."

Dad's eyes widen. "Oh."

I want to ask him so many things. Does he regret having bought those guns? Does he regret that he never talked to us about them? Does he still think it's okay for grown-ups to have guns? Does he think what happened was his fault?

But more than that, I want him to ask me questions. The questions he never asks. The questions that are more than just the simple "Are you okay?"

"You're a good girl, Quinn," Dad says, but he's not even looking at me. His shoulders are hunched. He's changed out of his work clothes, but he's still wearing his big shiny watch.

I should say something. I should ask him all my questions. I should make him ask me his. But I know I can't, so I kick the ball again and say, "Thanks, Dad."

FIFTEEN
CORA

I can't sleep. I try all my tricks. I recite the periodic table. I whisper the last line of *The One and Only Ivan* over and over again: "Mighty Silverback." I roll to my left side and then to my right.

Nothing works.

I keep trying not to look at Mabel's empty bed, but of course, I do. The morning she died, she'd left without making her bed. I was pretty annoyed by that, but I made it for her. The teal comforter is just how I left it. I haven't touched it since.

Mabel had all these messy habits, like leaving wet towels on the floor, eating Cheetos in bed and spreading the crumbs everywhere, and cluttering our shared nightstand with tubes of lip gloss. When she started high school, she got really into lip gloss because Grams finally allowed her to wear it to school.

Our nightstand is still cluttered with lip gloss tubes. I can't stand the idea of putting them away. But I also can't stand to look at them. When I see them, I think of that morning and the last things I ever said to her. My stomach hurts when I remember it.

Grams keeps telling me she thinks it would be healthy if we packed up Mabel's stuff. You know what else is healthy? Salad. My point? Just because something is healthy doesn't make it good.

I groan and slip out of bed. I turn on the light and drag the box from Quinn out from under my bed. I read through all the articles again and jot down notes in my journal.

Time travel is possible, I write.

Wormhole? I write. *Where do I find one?*

I think of the giant oak tree Quinn showed me. The articles do say that the best places to find a wormhole are places that are old and familiar. Forests are old, I guess. I don't know how familiar they are. Quinn's pretty familiar with the woods, though.

I grab my laptop and power it on. I type *wormhole* into the search bar and start reading everything that comes up. There are some helpful things like an article that explicitly states that forests are good places to find wormholes, but one thing I find makes me pause.

Some scientists hypothesize that time travel is the easiest between two points in time that aren't very far

from one another. For example, in accordance with
this theory, it would be easier to time-travel back two
days in time than it would be to travel back ten years.

I write down that whole chunk of text. It's almost October. In a little more than one month, it will be one year since it happened.

I think about how I felt sitting under the desk today during the drill. I don't want to feel helpless anymore—I want to do something. I reread everything I've written down.

Hypothesize. The word jumps out at me. That's it.

I turn my notebook to a blank page and write down the first step of the scientific method.

Make an observation, I write.

My sister is dead. I miss her so much.

The second part probably isn't necessary. A scientist like Dad would definitely trim it. I scratch it out.

Step two: Ask a question.

Can I time-travel to save Mabel? Can I save Mabel with science?

I flip back through my notebook. I reread the words of the MIT scientist. *Time travel is possible. It's very likely someone has already done it.*

Possible. Someone has already done it. My brain soaks up those words like a sponge. They are the proof I need to keep going.

Step three: Form your hypothesis.

I know as well as anyone that the success of a science experiment depends upon the hypothesis. A good hypothesis should include a couple of things. It must explain what you are going to test, and it also must set the scope for the project. Hypotheses help you to be organized, and they let you know what to expect from an experiment. They're also how you measure whether or not your experiment is successful.

Past hypotheses I've written have read like—

If we don't water our class plant, it will not grow.

If I drop the pennies in the lemon juice, they will become shinier.

If I launch a marble and a Ping-Pong ball from the same catapult, the Ping-Pong ball will travel farther.

Sometimes my hypotheses were right. Sometimes they were wrong. But it was okay no matter what. Those were simple experiments, though. This is not a simple experiment.

This time my hypothesis has to be right. It has to be perfect.

SIXTEEN
QUINN

Dear Parker,

Mom and Dad are still fighting every night. It makes me so sad to hear them argue. Mom thinks what you did is all Dad's fault. Dad thinks it's the fault of all the things you read on your computer.

I don't know what to think.

Actually, I do.

I think it was your fault.

Your sister,
Quinn

When I get the text from Cora telling me to meet her after school, I almost can't believe it. But when I walk to the side of the athletic field, she's already there, sitting on a bench, waiting for me.

"You're late," she says. She's wearing a knitted beanie over her dark curls and is looking down at a notebook that's spread out over her lap.

"School just let out."

"Ten minutes ago."

I swallow. "I waited in the library for the halls to clear out."

Her lips move like she's about to comment on that, but she doesn't. I rock back and forth on the balls of my feet and wait for her to say something. Anything.

"Aren't you going to ask me why I wanted to meet?" Cora doesn't look up from her notebook. She also doesn't offer me the seat next to her, so I stay standing.

"I—I—I—" A Freeze-Up. Great.

She finally looks up and blinks at me.

I blink back at her. Twice. *Freezing Up, but okay.*

"I think you might be right," she says. "About time-traveling."

My heart cartwheels.

"At first, I thought this was silly make-believe stuff. Like the things you were into when we were little," Cora says.

In my memory, both Cora and I liked setting up dinners for fairies that we made out of pebbles and moss and pretending to be wind spirits, racing quickly through our backyards, but I don't argue with her. I'm not about to start a fight.

"But this is really science," she continues. "And I owe it to Mabel to try."

In the distance, I can hear the smack of soccer balls moving through the air, and the muscles in the back of my ankles prick with a desire to be out on the field.

"Quinn?" Cora snaps. She's caught me daydreaming about soccer. "Are you even paying attention? This is important, you know."

"I know it's important." I'm relieved I'm able to find words so fast. "It was my idea in the first place."

Cora tilts her head to the side like she's weighing what I said. She plays with the end of one of her dark curls, her fingers climbing up the strand of hair like the spider from the old nursery rhyme we sang together in preschool.

"It was your idea, I know. But when I was talking, it seemed like you were somewhere else. Like you were distracted."

"I'm listening," I promise her.

"Okay," Cora says, and her mouth pinches with something that looks a little bit like satisfaction. "I think if we're going to do this, we need to structure the whole thing like a science experiment."

The word *science* always makes me think of diagrams and other boring things, but I try not to let my mind wander again.

"So all science experiments start with a question, right?"

I nod. That sounds vaguely familiar. I've never been able to keep all the steps of the scientific method straight. I mean, there are so many of them. If the whole thing is supposed to make the process easier, why do you need so many steps?

Cora keeps talking. "At first, I thought the question I was asking was 'Can I save Mabel by time-traveling?' But then when I went to write the hypothesis, I realized my question was lacking in scope."

"Lacking in scope," I repeat like I completely understand what she's talking about. Which I definitely don't.

"What I'm saying," Cora explains, "is that I realized I need to broaden it. The question I should've been asking is whether or not we can travel back in time to prevent Parker from hurting everyone, including himself."

My heart might've cartwheeled before, but now it's an Olympic gymnast, swinging from the high beams. Cora didn't have to add that last part of her sentence, but she did. She added it for me. I feel the sudden urge to hug her, but I stop myself.

Including himself. The fact she added that answers the question for me.

It's possible.

It's possible for things to be okay again.

Cora doesn't seem to realize how extraordinary what

she just said is because she keeps right on talking. "Step two is ask a question. It's also where the research part happens. And I did a lot of research last night."

"I did research, too," I add, my voice soft.

Cora gives me another weighing glance. It reminds me of the way Mom looks at fruit at the grocery store, always searching for unbruised peaches and bananas that are at perfect ripeness.

"Yes, well, I did further research. Which brings us to step three, the hypothesis."

I know I've barely spoken to Cora in almost a year, but if I know her at all, she already has a hypothesis.

"And I have a working hypothesis already."

Yup. I was right. I smile wide.

"What?" Cora says, her eyebrows arching.

"Nothing—I just—I'm gl-glad we're working on this together."

Cora's eyes narrow and her whole body stiffens. "I'm only doing this for Mabel."

Cora's words are like a hot slap across the face. I wince. "I know."

"I debated a lot about whether talking to you again was a betrayal of Mabel." Cora flips through her notebook and then holds it out so I can see the chart she made where she listed out the pros and cons of working with me.

"But I ultimately decided for a project this big, I need

a partner. And you are the obvious choice. I'm doing all of this for my sister, though. It's not about you."

I bite down hard on my bottom lip. "I know. I want to help Mabel, too. And everyone else."

I feel really guilty that, of the four people who died that day, I mostly think about Parker and Mabel. I wonder if that makes me a bad person. But I didn't know Jessica Ogden or Mrs. Isabelle Martinez (who was a ninth-grade science teacher at Chestnut High School.)

I've practiced saying their names aloud in the dark. I whisper them to Cupcake. And I know what they looked like because I read all about them online, even though Mom told me I shouldn't. Or rather, she banned me from looking them up. But I still did.

When I whisper their names, I visualize sending comfort to their families. I repeat the details I learned about them like how Jessica played the clarinet in the band and liked to volunteer at the animal shelter. And how Mrs. Martinez was the mom of a little boy and a talented long-distance runner, and enjoyed going bird-watching on weekends. I force myself to think about everything their families have lost because of Parker, but no matter how hard I try to concentrate, my mind always goes back to Mabel.

And to Parker.

That probably does make me a bad person. A familiar guilt swims around inside of me.

But if we fix this, if we really find that wormhole, maybe it will be okay that I didn't spend enough time thinking about Jessica or Mrs. Martinez. Maybe I'll be forgiven because I'll be saving them, too.

"Have you thought about when we want to time-travel back to?" I ask. "Isn't that the most important thing?"

Cora's posture stiffens again. "Yes," she says sharply. "Won't we just go back to that morning? Isn't that we're trying to stop? Besides, that morning makes the most sense. Since we weren't there when it happened, that means we won't risk running into other versions of ourselves, which would just make everything more complicated. You never want to run into your past self because that could have major time and space implications. You don't want to mess with the time continuum." She makes an exploding gesture with her hands.

Cora continues to ramble on about the technicalities of time travel, including the possibility of running into our past selves and why we want to avoid that all costs. While she talks, I think about my brother. I wonder if it's possible to stop him on that morning. That morning feels too late, but I can't bring myself to say it.

I know Mrs. Martinez died because she approached Parker. Mrs. Martinez was the last person to die before Parker took his own life. My skin goose-bumps with fear. I don't know if I can be as brave as Mrs. Martinez. Will I have the courage to stop Parker? To walk toward the thing I'm most afraid of instead of running away?

"Right," I say. I shake my head a little and try to pay attention to Cora.

"Okay. Let's not get distracted. It's very important that we follow the steps of the scientific method." Cora taps her finger against the notebook page for emphasis.

"The hypothesis," I say. That seems like the least important part to me, but I don't want to upset Cora.

"Right," Cora says, and starts to talk at length about all the things that make a good hypothesis. I only register half of it. I'm still thinking about coming face-to-face with my brother. I don't want to see the Parker from that morning. I want a Parker from earlier, the Parker he was before he changed—the Parker who held my hand in the ocean, the Parker who helped me get down from the tree, the Parker who taught me how to ride a bike. The Parker who used to sit with me on his bed, helping me sound out every word in my chapter book, patient when I got stuck on the *s*'s and *th*'s.

"Hey," I say, interrupting Cora.

She gives me a slightly sour look.

"You know what you said earlier? About how we're going to time-travel to stop Parker from hurting . . ." I stop talking for a moment and take a deep breath. "But he did something worse than hurt."

"I know." Cora's voice is barely above a whisper. It's

so light that the fall wind blowing across the athletic fields almost swallows it up. "I just can't say those other words. It's too hard."

I imagine the tiled floor of the science classroom. I've seen photos of it in the articles I read online. A cold sweat beads on the back of my neck. "This is all going to be hard. Really hard."

"I know that." Cora grits her teeth, and her eyes stick to mine like wet leaves on a windshield.

She doesn't say anything else, but she doesn't have to. We're making a promise.

We're going to do this together.

SEVENTEEN
CORA

The truth is, I wasn't so sure about the giant oak tree.

Quinn feels really strongly about it, though, and so I decided to roll with it. There's no scientific consensus on where exactly the best place to find a wormhole is. Dad says what you're looking for is scientific consensus. That means a group of scientists all agree on the same theory, which means the theory is probably right.

But for finding wormholes, there still isn't a scientific consensus. Some scientists recommend somewhere ancient (like Stonehenge in England, and that's out of the question for obvious reasons). Other scientists recommend somewhere familiar to you. And almost all the scientists use the term "exotic matter."

They say that's what you need to look for. That it's "exotic matter" that will open up the wormhole. The problem is, I can't get a precise definition of exactly what "exotic matter" is. It seems like something as made up as a "gut feeling" or "intuition."

So I guess that's why I agreed to follow Quinn's "intuition" about the giant oak tree.

I still have Junior Quiz Bowl practice on Mondays and Wednesdays and our meets on Thursdays, but every afternoon that I'm not busy, I've met Quinn in the woods. We've been working nearly constantly for two weeks. It's mid-October now, and the leaves have turned from silky green to leathery orange.

The change in color bothers me. It's a reminder that time is passing. That the wormhole is getting more and more difficult to find every day. Plus, when the leaves fall, they start to smell rotten. And they get muddy.

I'm what Grams calls an "indoor person." She used to ask me to help out in the garden, and I hated it. I don't like the feeling of dirt under my fingernails. Yuck.

So I'm trying my best to ignore the smell and mud as I sit on the ground by the trunk of the giant oak tree. Quinn and I are sitting back-to-back with our spines pressed up against one another.

When we were younger, me and Quinn would sit like this when she slept over in my house. I'd tell her about how chalk is made from microscopic plankton fossils (an awesome science fact if I do say so myself) and she'd tell me silly jokes she'd found on Popsicle sticks.

When we're sitting like this and I feel the bony, bumpy outline of her spine, it's like we're seven years old again. But we aren't seven years old. And we aren't swapping facts and jokes.

"He changed," Quinn says.

Recently, whenever I ask her about Parker, this is what she says.

"I know," I insist. "But how? Specifics are important."

She's quiet. I can't see her face, so I don't know if she's blinking.

"Like, tell me exactly how he changed," I add.

"I know what specifics are."

"It's just you were quiet."

"I was thinking. Not everyone thinks as fast as you." She squirms, and I press back against her harder. I don't want her to stand up. The realization of that surprises me, and I squeeze my hands together.

"Sorry," I say as gently as I can.

A wind blows through the forest. In all the books I'm assigned for English class, the wind is always described as a "howl" but I don't think that's the right word. A howl is a purposeful sound. It's a cry for help.

The wind that rustles the leaves is more aimless than that. I don't have patience for things that are aimless. I don't trust them.

"I'm not sure how to describe the specifics. It's like one day he was Parker. I mean, you knew Parker. And the next day, he wasn't," Quinn says.

At this, I squirm. I thought I knew Parker. He was Quinn's slightly goofy older brother. He was tall and thin with a hunched-over posture, almost as though he was embarrassed of his height. I try to think of what else I can remember about him. He used to build elaborate Hot Wheels tracks in Quinn's living room. He watched baseball games with her dad.

I never paid him much attention. I guess when we were younger I saw him a lot around Quinn's house. And when we got older, he was always in his room. I never thought too much about it, though. I always figured he just wasn't interested in hanging out with his younger sister and her friend.

My palms are sweaty, and I squeeze my hands together again.

"I guess. But I didn't really know him. He didn't talk to us much," I say.

"Not when he got older. When he changed."

"But how did he change?" I ask for what feels like the millionth time.

Albert Einstein says that the definition of insanity is doing the same thing over and over again and expecting a different result, but I know I need to keep asking her that question because the answer is important.

"Why does it matter?"

"You know why." I reach over to my side and grab my notebook. "The better we're able to visualize him, the more likely we are to be able to access the right wormhole."

"I can visualize him," Quinn says.

"Well, I need to be able to visualize him, too. Our visualization will be more powerful if I'm able to participate. And the more powerful it is, the more likely it is to succeed." I'm not quite sure that's true. That's an extrapolation from all the articles I've read. *Extrapolation* is a word Dad taught me. It basically means a guess based on the information you have. Almost all scientists make extrapolations based on the data they have. So that's what I'm doing, too.

"He started spending all this time by himself in his room. Whenever I'd check on him, he was on his computer. He started getting really mean, too."

I suck in a breath, reminding myself this is what I want. Information. "Mean how?"

"You know."

"No, I don't."

"I mean, it's like all of a sudden he decided he didn't like me. Most of the time, he acted like I didn't exist."

Quinn tenses, and I feel like an unstable chemical element whose electrons keep bouncing around. I think of the tube of dark red lip gloss on the nightstand. The unstable feeling inside of me grows.

When Mabel started high school, a distance opened up between us two. She kept telling me I wouldn't "understand" certain things. But that's one thing I've always been really good at. Knowing things. I didn't get why she would say that.

I don't like thinking about that distance now. I always thought things would go back to normal. That there would be lots of time to mend whatever had gotten messed up in our sister bond. You never think you're going to be out of time until you are.

"Did your parents notice that Parker was different?" I ask.

"I mean, they definitely knew. He would say awful things at dinner sometimes, and at first, Mom and Dad would argue with him. When he kept saying the things, they grounded him, but he didn't seem to care. He never wanted to go anywhere but his room anyway. Eventually, they stopped arguing with him. And stopped grounding him. It's like they got scared of Parker. Mom, especially. So she—I mean, we all stopped trying."

"What awful things?"

Quinn shakes her head. The end of her ponytail brushes against my back. "I don't want to say."

"You have to."

"I really don't want to, Core."

I reach for my notebook again, but she turns around and

117

grabs my hand to stop me.

She chews her bottom lip. We're sitting face-to-face now. I slowly pull my hand away from her.

"It's bad," she says.

"I know," I say. "I read the articles. I know all about the websites he used to leave comments on. The forums or whatever." I pick up a dead leaf and shred it between my fingers. When you remove the meat of a leaf, you're left with a skeleton hand.

"Then why are you making me talk about it?"

I don't look up at her. I stare at the mangled leaf in my palm. "Because I want to know what's true. Knowing the truth is important. I told you, the specifics are what are going to help us to visualize."

"Right, okay." Quinn says.

A question rolls around inside my brain. I'm scared to ask it, but I do anyway. "Did he go after Mabel because she was Muslim?"

Quinn's face drains of color. "I—I—I—I don't know. Mabel wasn't, I mean, you guys aren't even—"

I know she's trying to say that my family isn't *that* Muslim. Which is true. We're technically Muslim, but we aren't very religious people, but I'm not sure if that distinction would've mattered to Parker. Dad never taught Mabel or me much about Islam besides the basic things. He did tell us a lot about the achievements of Islamic scientists and mathematicians, though. I've always been proud of that history. There's a painting of the Dome of the Rock hanging in our kitchen. There's also one framed Quranic verse, written out in fancy calligraphy, but since I can't read Arabic, I always forget which one it is.

So who is Quinn to say what we are or what we aren't? I don't like when people say that because it makes me feel like they're telling me I'm not the kind of Muslim they're scared of. Like if I was more obviously religious, they'd have a problem with me. And that's all kinds of messed up. It's not fair that other people get to decide how much of something I am.

It's also messed up that when white boys like Parker commit a violent crime, everyone tries to figure out why they did it. Me included. But when a Black or brown kid does something like that, no one asks more questions. It's like they expected it of them or something. That makes me really mad.

Thinking about this makes me miss Mabel more. Mabel was the only other person who got it. Who was like me. Not Muslim enough, too Muslim. Not Arab enough, too Arab. We existed in our own in-between world. And now I'm left alone in it.

My face is growing hot and I can feel my throat closing up, so I force it open by talking. "The news said that Parker was active on all these forums full of people who hated women and immigrants and Muslims. And so I guess I'm wondering if he picked Mabel on purpose or if you think it was random."

When I'm done talking, I bring my knees to my chest. I've had that question for so long, but actually asking it out loud has given me serious chills.

"I don't know," Quinn says quietly.

I narrow my eyes. "How can you not know? He was your brother."

She hangs her head. "But I don't know, Core. By the end, I didn't feel like I knew him anymore at all."

"That doesn't make any sense. You should know."

Leaning to her side, she drags a finger through the dirt. "I know it doesn't."

My face is still warm. "It doesn't make any sense to me."

"It doesn't make any sense to anyone. Especially my family."

I know I should drop it, but I can't. "It should've made sense."

Mabel's death shouldn't have been random. It has to have meant something. It's so much worse for some reason if I think of it as being random.

Quinn's shoulders slouch and she chews on her bottom lip.

I jump up to my feet. "You want to know what I think? I think you should've stopped him."

Quinn stays seated in the ground. She doesn't say a

thing. She keeps dragging her fingers through the dirt.

"What are you doing? Aren't you going to say something?"

"I can't defend him, Core. I'm not going to defend him. I know I should've—" Her voice breaks. It's the first time I've seen Quinn cry. She blocks her eyes with her hands, trying to hide the tears from me, but I know they're there.

"I know," I say.

She removes her hands from her face. Her eyes are dry. I don't know how she manages to stop her tears so quickly. I can't do that.

"No. You don't. You don't know. And that's okay because you shouldn't know. But that's why I'm here." Quinn stands up. "To fix this. Because I know I should've done something before it happened—I just didn't know what. But now I'm here. And we're going to fix this, right?"

Part of me wants to say something mean. To make her hurt the way I'm hurting. I ball my fists at my sides. She should've done something earlier. I don't know what she could have done, but someone should've done something.

But the other part of me can't help but see Quinn McCauley, my best friend, looking miserable. That part of me wants to help her.

It wants to help us.

Then there's a third part that worries I'm a terrible sister because when I look at Quinn, my brain still thinks: *best friend*. It's like those two words are written in big block letters above her head, and no matter how hard I try to erase them, they won't go away. Of course I want Mabel back, but another awesome thing about this plan is that if it works, Quinn can be my best friend again.

It's hard to admit, but I've missed her. I've missed her so much. Tears brim at my eyes as I think about just how much I've missed her.

I relax my fists. "You're right. We have to just focus on fixing this. All of this."

Quinn paces around the giant oak tree. Her feet crunch over dead leaves as she makes quick circles. "Can I say something without you getting mad?"

"Sure." I don't know if I mean it or not.

"I know—" She starts but stops. She keeps walking in circles.

"You know?" I prompt.

"I know that you want to think of this like a science experiment, and before you say anything, I know why. It makes total sense. That's how it's going to work. And that's why I knew I needed your help because I knew I couldn't figure out the science stuff."

I mumble something, but she holds up her hand to shush me.

"I'm not done," she says.

"Okay."

"But I think you have to stop looking at this like it's a puzzle where you're collecting all the pieces. I know why you want as many details as you can get about Parker, but I think you have enough now. We've done the research part." She scrunches up her face in thought. "That was one of the steps, right?"

I nod, and I'm about to recite all the steps to her and clarify that really the research step came before the hypothesis, but before I can get that out, she starts talking again.

"But it seems like now is the time to try. I mean, why not just try? I think we're ready."

"Wait. You mean try? Like right now? To just do it? To time-travel?"

She shrugs. "Yeah. I don't think we need to do any more preparation. You're the one who always told me that the most amazing scientific achievements seemed almost like magic at first. That's what this is, right? A new scientific achievement."

I clench my jaw. "It's not magic. It's science."

"I know," she says quickly. Her pace has picked up. Circle after circle. It makes me dizzy to watch her.

"But it's going to feel like magic. And the thing I know about magic is that you have to look for it," Quinn says.

All of a sudden, she stops moving. She looks right at me. "Do you get what I'm saying? There's no equation to solve or puzzle piece to find. We've done that. Now there's only us and this tree."

I tilt my head to look up at the tree—its branches look like they are scraping the sky. I have so many questions, but when I look back at Quinn's face, I see an answer.

"Okay. You're right. Let's try."

EIGHTEEN
QUINN

Dear Parker,

You know how Mom loves to listen to old folksy songs by Johnny Cash and Joni Mitchell and Patsy Cline? I've noticed recently that in a lot of those songs the most powerful moment is actually when they stop singing. When everything is quiet except for the strum of a guitar or the jangle of piano keys.

But that silence says something. It makes you pay attention.

What I'm trying to say is, I've started to remember all the things you didn't say. The things you stopped saying, like "Hi" and "How are you?" and "I love you." And regular things like "Mom, can you buy more pickles?" and "Has anyone seen my blue sneakers? I can't find them."

125

That silence was loud. I wish I'd listened to it.

Your sister,
Quinn

I always find the school day hard to get through, but today was super tough. Every minute felt like it was being stretched into an hour. It was like someone pressed a button and put the whole day into slow motion.

But now I'm here and every single part of my body is racing.

I hear the sound of Cora's footsteps before I see her. She's never been a quiet walker.

"Hey," she says as she comes into view. She's wearing a thicker jacket than yesterday. It's flower-patterned corduroy and lined with fleece, and she's wearing another knitted hat that Grams probably made. This one's the color of a pea. "You beat me."

I rub my hands together. "I chanced the crowded hallways. I couldn't wait today."

She gives me a little smile. "You think this is really going to work?"

Overhead the sky is gray. It looks like a bedsheet that's been pulled tight at the edges. Like the type of sky that's waiting on something. I hope that something is the wormhole. I bow my head down and make a quiet and quick wish.

Inhaling, my lungs fill with the crisp and earthy air.

Everything around us is quiet and still. The only sound is the babble of the creek and the occasional gust of wind. I quickly cross the water and make it to the other side of the bank. It registers for me that Cora can now cross by herself. It makes me happy to think that I've taught her something.

Cora doesn't wait for me to answer her question. She walks right up to the trunk of the giant oak tree. She runs her fingers over the bumpy bark. "So you think the wormhole is just going to appear? Like right here?"

I walk to stand beside her. I bounce on the balls of my feet. It's impossible to stand still. "I'm not sure. But maybe it'll open up right there." I point at the bulge of bark that's high up on the trunk: the part of the giant oak tree that I call The Eyeball.

"You're obsessed with that spot."

I keep staring at it. "But doesn't it look magical?"

Cora smiles at me. "Science, not magic, remember?"

I smile back. "Okay. We're looking for science that feels magical. Is that better?"

"Yeah. I like that." Her smile widens and she tilts her head to look at the tree again. "Do you think we should climb up there?"

My mouth feels like its full of cotton balls. I do my best to push out my words. "I—I—I—I do-do-don't know. It's a hard tree to climb. I got st-st-stuck in it once."

Cora turns to me. "You mean before you showed me it?

When you were doing research on your own?"

I shake my head. "A long time ago." I don't tell her about Parker helping to get me down.

"We're looking for 'exotic matter,'" Cora says.

"I know. You keep saying that. I still don't understand what it is."

Cora wrinkles her nose. "I'm not sure anyone really understands what it is. It's like negative matter. But it's also, like, positive. It definitely exists." She pinches her fingers together for emphasis.

I smile again. "That sounds like magic dust to me."

Cora nudges my shoulder. "Maybe it is. And if it is, I'm thinking we should follow your gut."

"Did you, Cora Hamed, really just tell me to follow my gut?"

Cora's smile widens. It feels so good to see her smile. Really smile. It makes me forget all about my cotton-balled mouth. "Yes, and I'm absolutely mortified by it. But I'm willing to go to great lengths to find 'exotic matter.'"

"Me too." I go back to staring at The Eyeball. This has to work. It just has to.

"So let's climb it."

A shadowy pit opens up inside me. Sometimes when I think about Parker, my memories feel like quicksand. It's so easy to get stuck in them. I stare at the giant oak tree and remember Parker's steady hands guiding me down, how faraway the ground seemed, what a relief it was when my feet touched down, how I could feel his heartbeat through his hand, and how I didn't let go of him for even one second.

"I—I—I don't know."

"Come on," Cora urges. "You'll have to show me how, though."

"I mean, it's not that com-com-complicated. It's climbing a tree."

"You said you got stuck."

I shrug, trying to shake away my quicksand-like memories. "Yeah, because this tree is kind of hard. But climbing a tree is climbing a tree."

"Says the girl who climbs trees."

"Says the girl who gets an A on every single test."

Cora puts her hands on her hips. It's not nice, but I've always felt like she looks kind of snotty when she does this. I don't think in my whole life I've ever put my hands on my hips. It's things like this that used to make Scarlett and Ainsley say that Cora was stuck-up. That and how she's always correcting people by blurting out random facts. Whenever anyone said something bad about Cora, I always defended her, but probably not enough.

"Tests are really different than trees," Cora says. She doesn't take her hands off her hips.

"Probably," I agree.

She dramatically slides one arm out in front of her. "So show me."

I'm about to argue some more, to tell her that I'm not sure we have to climb it to find the wormhole, but the more I look at The Eyeball, the more it calls to me.

The gray sky overhead cracks open and a sliver of sunlight streams down. It bounces right off The Eyeball. My legs turn to Jell-O and my heart thuds inside my chest, hammering against my rib cage.

"Do you see that?" Cora says, pointing right at the speck of light. "Is that the start of the wormhole?"

A shiver creeps up my spine. "Maybe," I whisper, scared that if I speak too loud, whatever it is will go away—that magical shimmering.

I take one more big gulp of the fresh air and then jump up and grab a low branch. I swing myself up to the next one and bend over and extend my hand to Cora. I bounce on the branch to make sure it's sturdy. It gives a little, but I can tell it will hold me.

"Wow," Cora says, gripping my hand. "You're good at this."

I offer her a sheepish smile. I want to say something smart, something that will impress her more, but I know the best thing I can do is get us up to The Eyeball.

I climb to the next branch and then turn around to offer her my hand. We move higher and higher like this—I climb and then I pull her up. Eventually we make it high enough that I can reach out and touch the bumpy surface of The Eyeball.

The pale watery sunlight is still glinting off it. I push my fingers into the bark, searching for a hidden nook. A key. Anything that will open up the wormhole. Twisting my wrist, I pretend to grab the brass doorknob that I've been imagining.

Cora perches beside me and lets out loud, uneven exhales. She's stiff and holding tightly on to the branch and staring down with wide eyes at the forest floor.

"It's okay," I say.

"I know," she says, but I can hear a swallow of hesitation in her voice.

We sit there quietly for a moment. I keep staring at The Eyeball, hoping that something miraculous is just going to happen. I hope for it so hard that I can feel every muscle inside of me straining, reaching out to the giant oak tree, begging it to reveal the wormhole that I know it holds.

"So," Cora says. "We should probably start the visualization."

"The visualization. Right."

Cora's lips pull into a straight line. "Don't say it like that."

"Sorry."

"It's real science, Quinn. I read about it. The visualization is a key part."

I nod. I trust her, but still. It feels like the wormhole door should just open. I reach out and knock on The Eyeball. My heart sinks when nothing happens.

"It doesn't work like that." I can hear the impatience in Cora's voice. "It's important to follow the correct steps."

"Okay, okay," I say. I settle back on the branch.

"Should we sit spine-to-spine?"

I glance down at the ground. The leaves look impossibly tiny. "Do you think that's a good idea? We don't want to lose our balance."

"Come on," Cora insists. "We have to do everything we can."

"You really think it will make a difference?"

She considers this. After a few beats of silence, she says, "Yeah. I do."

"Okay." I slowly turn my back to her. I use my hands to grip the branch below me, almost as though it were a horse's saddle. The only time I've ever ridden a horse in my whole life was when I visited Gammie and Papa in North Carolina. Parker rode along beside me. "You're holding on, right?"

"Yeah, Quinn. I'm holding on." Cora makes a clicking sound with her tongue.

"What's that?" I say.

"Shhh. I'm resetting our environment so it's clear that we're starting our summoning ritual."

Summoning ritual. Those words float around in my

head. I like the way they sound—official. And magical. I hold my breath and suck in all the belief I can muster. *This will work, this will work, this will work.* The chant pounds inside of me.

"Okay," Cora says slowly. "We're both going to visualize that morning." She's quiet, and I think it's time to start, but then she adds, "The science classroom."

I close my eyes and try to draw up the pictures from the news articles that I wasn't supposed to read. I always thought that was such a ridiculous rule. My brother had done this horrifying thing, but Mom and Dad thought that reading about it was what was going to cause problems.

I struggle to hold an image of the science classroom. The long lab tables with their black laminate tops and metal sinks, the unlit Bunsen burners in the center, the milk crate filled with freshly polished glass instruments. Usually my mind is good at drawing pictures. It's like the only thing it's good at, but for some reason, I'm not able to do it right now.

I see the science classroom, but then it flickers away, and I'm in the narrow upstairs hallway of my house, where the walls are painted a runny-yolk yellow. I'm inside the memory of a specific afternoon.

Mom and Dad were both at work. When I heard Parker's footsteps, I came out of my room to see what he was doing. Those days it was rare for him to leave his room, and I'd stupidly thought that maybe he was coming to talk to me.

But he wasn't.

Without any effort at all, my mind flashes to an image of Parker's back, his curved shoulders and loose-fitting jeans with the brand label on the waistband tag. He stomped toward my parents' bedroom and I quietly tiptoed after him. I willed him to turn around and see me, but he didn't.

I stood in the doorway and watched him head to the corner of Mom and Dad's bedroom, the place where Dad's safe was. I knew Dad had guns because he would sometimes go hunting on the weekends with his friends, but he had never talked to me about where he stored them.

Parker fumbled with the safe's lock. It wasn't until the door to the safe swung open that I realized what was happening. That those were Dad's guns.

I let out an audible gasp, and Parker spun around to face me. His eyes sparked with anger, and—

"It's not working, is it?" Cora's voice pulls me back into the present.

Wait! I was there. I traveled there. I did it. Did I? My heart races. I grip the rough bark of the branch, and a splinter of wood cuts into my fingernail bed. I slowly open my eyes. The forest comes back into view. The bumpy moss-covered bark of the giant oak tree, the ground full of rust-colored leaves. The gurgle of the creek.

I didn't. I'm here. I can feel Cora's back rise and fall slowly with her breaths.

"It didn't work," Cora says, and the disappointment in her voice hurts so much that I pick at the wood splinter, looking for another kind of pain to distract me.

Guilt sloshes around inside of me. Maybe it didn't work because I didn't picture the right moment. Maybe instead of picturing the science classroom, Cora also should've been visualizing the moment that I was. The moment when I knew something was really wrong. The moment when I could've stopped my brother.

But she doesn't know to try to picture that because I haven't told her about it. I haven't told anyone.

I open my mouth to tell her, to tell her the truth. But I can't find the words. They slip away from me like smoke ribboning from an extinguished candle. Every time I reach for them, they disappear.

Cora's spine pulls away from mine. The branch we're sitting on bobs up and down as she turns around. I turn around, too, slowly. She looks unsteady, and I instinctively reach my arm out and put it on her knee. I won't let her fall.

Her eyes are darting all around. I want her to look at me. I'm hoping she'll see the guilt that I'm drowning in, and she'll know. She'll force me to tell her. But she keeps looking past me.

"We must be missing something," she says.

I follow her eyes. They're staring at The Eyeball. The glimmer of sunlight is gone. The sky is a gray that is as heavy as cement. It doesn't look like it holds even a pinch of magic.

"Yeah," I say, my voice low and tangled.

"I just don't know what it could be."

I squirm a little.

"Do you have any ideas?"

Yes, my brain thinks. "No," my mouth says.

Cora's face is like a crumpled-up piece of paper, all of her features squeezing together. "I'll have to do more research tonight. There has to be something we're missing. There has to be."

I don't say anything. Straining my ears, I listen for the chirping of birds, but I don't hear a thing. I can only hear the rushing of the creek water.

"Life," I whisper without realizing it.

Cora's attention snaps to me. "What?"

"What you told me about birds. That when we hear them, it means there's water, which means there's life."

Cora smiles a little. But her face doesn't look anything like happiness. "You remember that?"

"I remember everything you tell me."

She rolls her eyes, but her smile grows. "Whatever."

"I do."

"Then remember this: We're going to do this, okay?" Her eyes lock with mine.

We make a visual pinkie promise. "Promise," I say, choking back another wave of guilt.

Cora tilts her head to the ground. "Um, how are we going to get down?"

"Let me help you," I say, and slowly move to a lower branch.

I hold my hand out to her, and she takes it.

NINETEEN
CORA

I haven't gotten a lot of playing time this Quiz Bowl match. Coach Pearlman has massively favored the eighth graders on our team, which makes sense because Streamwood always has a good team, and we really need to beat them if we want a chance at qualifying for the regional playoffs.

Each match is made up of three rounds. Streamwood already won the first one, and by the end of the second round, it's clear that they're probably going to handily beat us. So that's when he decides to let Mia and me have a shot.

He subs me in for Peter, and Mia in for Molly. Owen's still riding the bench while Nora Cheng sits sandwiched between Mia and me, the sole eighth grader left.

The first couple of questions breeze by. Nora reaches for the buzzer a couple of times, but she doesn't get the question right either time. Mia casts me a nervous look, and I give her an apologetic shrug.

I know I should be trying harder, but my brain can't focus on this right now. I stayed up until two a.m. last night reading the entire internet. I wish that was an exaggeration, but it's not. I watched every video on YouTube about wormholes, even the really silly ones with the added-in special effect sounds. I read every thread on every forum. And I scrolled through Every. Single. Comment.

My eyes are bleary and my head aches, and I still haven't figured out what Quinn and I did wrong. The only thing that's bringing me any comfort is that several of the things I read mentioned that it usually takes some time to coax a wormhole out of the universe.

The man who is asking the questions clears his throat. He's a math teacher at Streamwood Middle School. I wasn't paying attention when he said his name at the beginning of the match. It's a home meet for Streamwood, so our team rode the bus to their school.

Away matches are not my favorite. They make me nervous. I'm not familiar with the schools, so I don't know where all the exits are or how to get out quickly if I need to.

"The next category is Amphibians," says the man whose name I don't know.

Mia looks over at me. I don't meet her gaze, though. I ignored her the whole bus ride here, and I know she's already pretty annoyed at me. The thing is, I knew I wouldn't be able to talk to her about anything other than wormholes. I used to pride myself on being able to think about multiple things at once. Grams says I've always been an excellent multitasker.

But these days, I've lost all my multitasking abilities. It's like my brain is a replicating strand of DNA that just won't quit. I'm only able to think about time travel.

"The definition of an amphibian is—"

Nora reaches for the buzzer. She's fast—I have to give that to her. She looks at both Mia and me.

"A cold-blooded vertebrate?" she whispers to us.

"I don't know," Mia says.

"That sounds right to me." I give her a nervous shrug.

"A cold-blooded vertebrate," she answers.

"That's correct," the Streamwood Middle School math teacher announces. He marks down a point for our team. We're still behind by a lot, but it feels good to get on the board.

The round continues. Nora keeps reaching for the buzzer. Mia sometimes even hits it, too. I never reach out for it. I'm trying really hard to focus, but my brain doesn't even register the questions.

Coach Pearlman catches onto my slack. He subs back in Peter. I hang my head as I walk over to sit back down at the table next to Owen.

"Are you okay?" Owen whispers. He stretches his long legs out in front of him, the khaki uniform pants inching up to reveal his koala-patterned socks.

I nod. I don't quite trust my voice.

He glances at me. "You sure?"

It's not like Owen to push. I cross my arms over my chest. "Yeah. I'm fine."

"You seem different. Like not just today, but recently."

I can't quite look at him. I'm worried my stomach will go all fizzy, and that would be too much right now.

"Don't worry about it," I say.

"Okay. Whatever you say." Owen turns away from me and puts in his earbuds. Coach won't be happy if he catches him listening to music during the match, but I guess that's not my problem.

I sort of want Owen to say something else. But I don't know what. The not knowing is the worst feeling of all. I look over at him a few times, but he doesn't look back.

When the match is over, we all line up to shake hands. Some of our team is riding back home on the bus, but the rest of us are going home with our parents, who came to watch. Dad wasn't able to make it to this one, but I spot Grams at the back of the classroom and head toward her, when Mia taps my shoulder.

"What?" I say.

"That's exactly what I'm saying to you," Mia says.

I spot Mia's mother standing next to Grams. Mrs. Tolentino is dressed in a gray suit. She works at a law firm downtown and looks like she came straight here from the office.

"Huh?" I say.

"I'm saying 'What?' because something is seriously going on with you. You didn't even try." She points at the space near the front of the classroom, where the match took place. "You totally blew it."

"I tried," I mumble. My brain still feels cloudy and cramped.

"Did you?"

"Why are you blaming our loss on me? That's not fair." She scowls at me. "That's not what I'm saying."

"Then what are you saying?"

"That something is up with you, and it seems like the only person you're willing to talk to is Quinn McCauley." Mia's white face flushes red at the mention of Quinn's name, and I can feel my own skin heating up, too.

"I thought I was supposed to be your best friend. You can tell me things, you know." She leans in close to me. Her natural deodorant smells like coconuts and eucalyptus. "Like are you talking to her about Owen? Do you think it's weird to talk to me about it because Owen and I are friends, too?"

I gape at her. I am most definitely not talking to Quinn about Owen. But I'm definitely not talking about it with Mia either. "It's none of your business."

She puts a hand on her hip. "I'm your best friend."

"Says who?" I blurt out.

She steps away from me as her eyes narrow. "Excuse me?"

I know I should apologize. I should back down. But I don't. "I've never said that you're my best friend."

Mia's face has turned beet red, and the tips of her ears are the shade of a fire engine. "So that's it? You are back to being best friends with Quinn?"

"This isn't about Quinn." I try to keep my voice steady, but I can hear the cracks in it.

"Whatever. It clearly is. You've been spending every day hanging out with her." Mia slides her foot out in front of her and drags a slow line across the shiny classroom floor like she's trying extra hard to delineate something. "You know, I'm pretty tired of your act."

"My act?"

"Yeah. Your act. Like you want everyone to feel sorry for you because of what happened to your sister. And we all do feel bad, but you can't just go around and treat us all like we don't matter."

The heat in my face is growing. I'm sure I'm almost as red as Mia. I stare down at my shoes. I want to tell her a hundred things, but I only shake my head.

"Whatever," she repeats. "Friends tell each other things, Cora. They don't keep secrets from one another."

I open my mouth to respond, but Mia's mom comes up behind her. She gives Mia's shoulder a gentle squeeze.

"You girls okay?" Mia's mom asks. Since Mia cut her

hair short, the two of them look even more alike with their matching angled bobs, sharp cheekbones, and wide steely-blue eyes.

"We're fine," Mia says, glaring at me to let me know that everything is absolutely not okay.

"I know it was a disappointing result, but you two did well." Her hand stays planted on Mia's shoulder. Mia's mom's fingers are perfectly manicured and painted with a light pink polish. I don't know if my mother ever got her nails done.

Those are the type of questions I was once able to ask Mabel. Mabel didn't know the answers, but she liked to pretend she did. She was the only person who didn't squirm at the mention of my mother.

Now there's no one.

I never even ever really missed my mother or the idea of her. It was more like a curiosity. Something to wonder about with my sister. But ever since Mabel died, I've found myself missing everything. Even things I never missed before.

Mia keeps giving me a sullen look. She mumbles something, and her mom gives me an almost-apologetic wave goodbye. "We will see you later, Cora. Have a good night."

Grams is still waiting at the back of the classroom. I grab my backpack and we walk to the car in silence.

As Grams pulls out of Streamwood Middle School's parking lot, she says, "So are you going to tell me what that was all about?"

I kick my feet against the back of the passenger seat.

"Cora London," Grams says. "Stop that. You aren't a toddler."

I frown, but I stop kicking. Grams isn't to be messed with.

"Thank you," she says. I can feel her watching me through the rearview mirror. Grams's eyes have a weight to them—you always know when they're on you. "So talk to me."

"There's nothing to say. We had a bad match."

"I don't think that's what's on your mind. I saw you quarreling with Mia."

"Quarreling," I repeat.

"Fighting. You know."

"I know what 'quarreling' means."

"I know you do, sassafras. I'm asking you what was going on between the two of you. I saw that mess with my own two eyes."

"You did, huh?"

"Cora London," she says again. "Don't be smart."

"You know, you're always telling me all these things not to be. But you never tell me what to be." I stare out the window. The sky is a deep-purple color. On another night, I might think it looks pretty. Tonight, though, it reminds me of a bruise. I press my finger against the chilly window.

"No one should tell you what to be."

"Well, I'm tired of hearing what I can't be."

"Hm." She drops it for a few moments, but soon enough, she's back at it. "So what is Mia so mad about?"

"That I don't know a lot about amphibians," I grumble.

"I heard Quinn's name."

I sink down into my seat. I wonder why of all the grandmas in the world I got the one with superhero hearing. "Jeez. Spy much?"

"You were quarreling in an open room."

"An open room? It was a private discussion."

"Well, could've fooled me. You were having it out in front of everyone."

The purple is darkening to black. I watch the houses as we zoom by them. The lights in the windows—all the people inside. I wonder how many of them are missing sisters. Or mothers. Missing someone. Anyone. My missing sometimes makes me feel like the loneliest person in the world.

"Cora London?"

"Yes?"

"Are you simply going to flat-out ignore me, honeybee?"

"I don't feel like talking."

"Yeah, but you need to talk, baby girl. You know I only push and prod you because I love you, right?"

"I miss her," I say, and I can feel the tears collecting in the base of my throat. "I miss her so much."

"I know you do, baby," Grams says softly. "We all do."

I wipe my eyes, but it doesn't help. More tears come. This is the trick with Grams. She starts out tough. She never talks to you like you're a little kid. And somehow that toughness chips at you until you become doughy enough to talk. I never think it's going to work, but it almost always does. And once you are dough, she softens.

"I think I might be a bad sister because I'm talking to Quinn again."

"No, honeybee. You aren't a bad sister."

"How do you know that?"

At the next red light, I meet her eyes in the rearview mirror. Grams and I have the same eyes. It's the only physical feature we share. She says they're my mom's eyes, but I like that they come from her. Mabel had the same eyes, too. It was something we all shared.

"Maybe I don't know. Maybe I just think."

"That doesn't make any sense. You can't think something you don't know."

"Sure you can."

The tears sting my eyes. "Well, that isn't comforting. I want you tell me I'm not a bad sister. Can you at least do that?"

"You aren't a bad sister, baby. You've never been a bad sister, not one day in your life." She lets out a deep sigh and steers the car through a sharp turn. "But have you ever thought that maybe it's okay to sometimes not know things?"

I stare out the window. I wrap my arms around myself and keep looking outside for answers.

TWENTY
QUINN

Dear Parker,

Did you know I draw? I used to only draw pictures in my mind, but I've started to actually sketch things on paper.

I can't tell if I'm any good at it yet, but I like it.

I keep thinking about what I would draw for you if I had the chance.

Your sister,
Quinn

The air today smells cold and stiff. It feels inflexible, which I don't think is a good sign, but I try to push that thought away.

I shove my hands into the pocket of my coat as I head toward the giant oak tree. Cora won't be there this afternoon, but I still want to pay it a visit on my walk home.

Most of the trees have lost all their leaves now, making it easier to see across the whole forest preserve. Maybe that's how loss always is. It helps you better see what was already there. What was always there.

In the distance, I spot the thick trunk of the giant oak tree looming. Its branches are almost bare now, too. They curl out against the gray sky like they're looking for a hug.

I carefully hop from large rock to large rock, crossing the creek. Cold water splashes against my ankles, soaking into my socks. I don't mind it too much.

I walk right up to the giant oak tree. I stare hard at The Eyeball. The scale of the giant oak tree gets lost the closer I get to it. When I'm far away, I can see how much taller it is than almost every other tree. But when I get close to it, I lose all perspective.

As I approach, the air around me feels less frozen. It's almost as though the magic of the giant oak tree melts some of the cold away. I reach my hand out, half expecting to touch something, but I don't find anything.

The guilt inside me is tangled and twisted, like necklaces tossed together carelessly. The truth is probably the key, the secret that will make all of this work. I know I need to tell Cora, but that feels even more impossible than finding a wormhole.

Just show me I'm right about you, I beg the tree.

Its dark bark is slick with last night's rain. The moss is slimy as I touch my palm to it. I'm begging so hard that I can feel my longing rattling around inside of me, but it doesn't seem to have any effect on the tree.

It just stands there. As still as ever.

The sky splits open, and a cold rain drizzles down. The rain drops on my head as I circle the tree, staring up at The Eyeball. The rain grows heavier, and finally, I shout, "So you're really going to make me tell her? Is that what you want? If I tell her, will you show us the wormhole?"

My voice is drowned out by the rain. The tree doesn't answer. A slice of lightning cracks overhead, and I jump, my skin goose-bumping all over. I stare at the cracks of light, fracturing across the sky. The bright spots against the darkness.

TWENTY-ONE
CORA

"You seem different today," Dr. Randall says, and the essential oil diffuser lets out a loud puff. The room fills with the scent of eucalyptus.

I squeeze my hands together. Sometimes I worry that in psychology school Dr. Randall learned how to actually see the inside of people's brains. What I mean is that I worry he always knows exactly what I'm thinking, and he's just sitting there waiting to see if I'll tell him. Or if I'll lie.

Objectively, I know that's not true. I still worry about it, though.

Right now, I'm worried that he knows I'm not telling him about my time-travel plan. He keeps looking at me like he capital-K Knows. I shift in my seat and stare at the diffuser. I also wonder if Dr. Randall ever gets sick of the smell of eucalyptus.

He arches his graying eyebrows. "Does my observation make you uncomfortable?"

I squeeze my hands together again. "Not particularly."

He makes his signature "mmm" sound. "You're more reluctant to talk than usual, but you also seem more, dare I say, sure-footed."

"Sure-footed?"

He turns to the clock. "Our time is almost up, and you haven't cried once today."

"Is that bad? Do you take that as a personal failing?"

He leans back in his big plushy chair and laughs a little. "No. I actually am choosing to take it as a point of pride. That you're getting better adjusted, finding your feet. Hence, sure-footed."

Dr. Randall talks to me in a sophisticated way. It's like he knows I can handle all the fancy loops of his speech patterns. Which I can. Definitely.

"You told me before there's nothing wrong with crying."

"There is nothing wrong with crying. But, to me, the fact that you aren't crying is also a good sign. Two things can be true, you know."

I look around his office. There's a large abacus in the middle of the floor with multicolored beads. I know his younger patients play with toys while they talk to him. When we first met, he asked if I'd like to squeeze a ball or push the beads on the abacus. I declined. I'm not five years old, after all—but now the abacus looks pretty appealing. It would at least be something for my hands to do.

"Cora, I hope you know that you can ask me anything," he says.

"How do you know I want to ask you something?"

Another "mmm." A patient smile. "Just a hunch."

"You said two things can be true. But do you think impossible things can be true?" The question spills out of my mouth.

Dr. Randall doesn't seem flustered by it, though. "Well, the word *impossible* suggests something that is untrue. But I want you to clarify what you mean by 'impossible.'"

"Impossible," I repeat.

"Impossible," he confirms. He eyes me, waiting. Dr. Randall is very good at waiting.

"Like time travel?"

"Time travel." He says those two words like they are the most neutral things in the whole world. "You've been thinking a lot about time travel?"

I squirm. I don't make eye contact with him. I find it very difficult to lie to Dr. Randall. "Not a lot."

"What appeals to you about time travel?"

I look up. "Isn't it obvious?"

"You want to change what happened to your sister?" He tips forward in his chair.

I nod and fold my arms. "Obviously."

"What would you change?"

"I wouldn't want her to—"

Dr. Randall raises his hand. "Obviously." He uses my word gently. "I'm asking, is there something particular you would change?"

I squint, unsure of what he's asking.

His face is wide open. I don't know how he does that. He gives off the impression that he would be as easy to read as *See Spot Run*, but whenever I try, it's like I'm looking at an ancient Latin text or something—indecipherable. "Is there something in particular you maybe regret from your last moments with Mabel? Something you would change?"

My stomach clenches as I think about that last morning with Mabel. The lip gloss. The fight. This is something I haven't talked about with Dad or Grams. I definitely haven't told Quinn.

Dr. Randall waits for me to talk. He holds his pose like statue.

"I got in a fight with Mabel. The morning it happened." I look down at my hands.

Dr. Randall makes his "mmm" sound. It's softer, though. "What was the fight about?"

"Argument might be a better word."

"Words are important to you. Aren't they, Cora?"

I shrug. "I like to be specific."

He nods. "That's a good thing."

"I think so. Some people don't, though."

He gives me a tight smile like he understands what I mean by that. "Was your argument with Mabel about being specific?"

My eyes drop to the carpet. It's a plush beige. It's always clean. I can never even find a fleck of dirt. Dr. Randall must vacuum a lot. "It was about the fact she—" I stop talking. "It doesn't matter."

"Hm. I think it's important to you, and therefore, it matters," Dr. Randall says.

I take a deep breath. "It was like high school changed her. She'd only been there a little more than two months, right?" I know the exact amount of time Mabel was in high school, sixty-five days, two hours, three minutes. But I don't volunteer that information.

"But she'd already changed? How?"

"It's like all of a sudden I was her little sister instead of just her sister."

"Weren't you her little sister?"

"Yeah. I guess. But I really became her little sister when she started high school. She kept saying things like 'Oh, you wouldn't understand.' Mabel never had said stuff like that to me before. She always talked to me about everything. She never made me feel silly for asking questions. But that fall, she was different." Even as I talk, I can feel my whole body resisting it. These aren't things I should say out loud. This is a betrayal of my sister.

"And that upset you? Is that why you fought?" Dr. Randall asks. His face is as calm as ever.

"She got all these new lip glosses. Grams didn't want us wearing makeup until we started high school. Honestly, Grams wasn't a big fan of Mabel wearing makeup even when she started high school, but that had been the deal. And Mabel started waking up early and spending all this time in the bathroom getting ready for school. That morning, she came back into our room, and she had this dark shade on." I keep staring at the very clean carpet. I don't want to see Mabel's face—her dark lips, the expression on her face when I insulted her.

Dr. Randall lets out an even breath, but he doesn't say anything.

I stretch my legs out. They don't hit anything, only air. "And I told her the lip gloss looked ugly, okay? I told her that. It was a mean thing to say. And it's the last thing I ever said to my sister. Are you happy now?"

He shakes his head a little. "I'm not happy. But I'm glad you told me. I can see this is bringing you a lot of pain. It's a very common occurrence that we regret the final moment we had with a loved one. Of course, we never expect it's going to be the last time. And in your case, you certainly didn't expect it would be the last time."

My throat feels like it's filled with acid. "She didn't make her bed that day, either. I made it for her. And I was mad at her. While she was being killed, I was mad at her. Can you believe that?"

My crying switch flips on. Tears slide down my face.

Dr. Randall nods again. "You're going to have to learn to let go of your regret, Cora. You can't hold on to it forever."

The thing is, though, I'm pretty sure I can. I'm pretty sure I could hold on to it until the end of time.

But hopefully I won't have to because I'm going to change everything. Quinn and I are going to find that wormhole, and I have a list of the first things I'm going to say to Mabel:

You can always talk to me about anything. I'll try my best to get it. And if I don't, I promise I won't ask too many questions.

Your lip gloss looks cool.

I love you more than anything.

And it's okay if you never make your bed. I'll always make your bed as long as it means you're here.

Those are the things I should have said that morning, but those aren't the things you say to your sister when you're mad at her. Those aren't the things you say until you realize that the world is a place where sisters sometimes don't come home from school.

It's going to feel so good to get to say those things to her. I can practically taste the words on my lips.

"You're smiling," Dr. Randall says.

I guess I am.

"Are you forgiving yourself, Cora?"

I squirm. I don't like lying to Dr. Randall. "Forgiveness is, like, an impossible thing, right?"

"I suppose."

"But it's also possible. It's a thing that seems impossible, but it is possible."

Dr. Randall smiles. He actually smiles. The rareness of it feels like witnessing a solar eclipse. "I like that."

"Me too," I say, and spend the rest of the session thinking about how to make an impossible thing—The Impossible Thing—possible.

When our time is up, Dr. Randall rises to his feet and says, "Okay. That's it for today. I'll see you next week, Cora."

I give him a wave. This might be the last time I ever see him because if I find the wormhole, I'm going to be living in a world where I don't need to see Dr. Randall anymore. That thought makes my heart soar. I give him a big smile. I want him to know how much he helped me.

"Goodbye," I say as I walk out of his office

TWENTY-TWO

QUINN

Dear Parker,

What happened to your friends? Joe and Anderson and the others? They used to sometimes come over to our house. I can't really remember the last time I saw them. It wasn't something I thought a lot about, until it happened.

Did you guys stop being friends before you did it? You seemed so alone that whole fall. I could tell you were lonely, but I didn't know what to do. After it happened, no one said they were your friend. I don't blame them.

I didn't want to be your sister either.

But I also wanted you back.

That doesn't make much sense. None of it makes sense.

Your sister,
Quinn

By the time I reach home, I'm soaked.

"Quinn," Mom says, greeting me right when I come in the door. "Are you okay? Where have you been?"

My shoes leak muddy water onto the freshly mopped floor. "Just walking home."

Mom takes my wet jacket from me. "I could've picked you up."

The smell of something warm and buttery wafts through the air. I turn my face to the kitchen. "What are you making?"

"Pies!" Mom says. "Come see!"

In the kitchen, there are five different pies cooling on the island. Patsy Cline is crooning on the speakers and there are about a dozen mixing bowls in the sink.

"Wow. You've been busy."

Mom gives me a smile, and it's a real one. Not her lemony one, but an expression that looks as sweet as the cooling pies. "Well, I got it in my head today. I was thinking about how lovely it would be to open up my own bakery. And then the more I thought about it, I was thinking that shop could feature pies specifically. Of course, we'd have other items, but pies would be the main attraction. And then I was like, 'I should make some to see if I could do it.'"

I stand on my tip toes to get a better look at one of the pies. The golden-brown top has an elaborate crisscross pattern. I don't know what the proper name is for that technique. "You want to open a pie shop?

Mom plays with the back string of her apron. "Well, maybe."

"Does that mean we'd move? Like Dad wants to?"

Mom's sugary smile disappears. "What? No. Why would you say that?"

"Because . . ." I can feel everything I've been trapping inside of me slosh, like the way you feel when you've drunk too much water too quickly and it slides all around your rib cage.

She bends down to give me a patient look. Even though I know she doesn't want this conversation to continue, she's been trained over the years to be encouraging when it takes me a minute to find my words.

"Because Dad wants to move. And that's something we should talk about. And we should also talk about all the things we never talk about. Like why he wants to move," I say, my words slow but steady.

"Oh, Quinn," Mom says. She looks away, moving to go check the oven even though I know there's nothing in it.

"I'm serious, Mom." This conversation is an uphill climb, but I'm finally finding my footing. I imagine myself scaling a mountain, pushing upward, bit by bit. I take a breath. "We should talk about it. We've never talked about how Dad had those guns. About—"

162

"Quinn!" Mom's voice is sharp like broken glass. "Stop."

I grip the kitchen island counter, curling my fingers underneath it. "Why? Why can't we talk about it?"

Her bottom lip trembles. "You're too young. It's not something to—"

The guilt inside me isn't sloshing anymore. It's overflowing. I can't hold it in any longer.

"I'm too young? I'm not too young to have people stare at me all day at school because of what Parker did."

Mom's face has hardened into a metallic-looking surprise. I never interrupt her. Never. Ever. I never interrupt anyone.

"Quinn. Don't speak about your brother like—"

"Like what, Mom? Parker did it. He killed people. And we need to talk about it. We need to talk about why he did it. We need to talk about how it happened. We need to talk about Dad's guns and how Parker changed and we need to—" My throat is filled with bile. I want to keep talking, but I'm forced to stop to swallow. It's only when I taste the salt on my lips that I realize I'm crying.

I reach out and touch my cheeks. I haven't cried in so long. I haven't let myself.

"Oh, Quinn," Mom says. Her face is steelier than steel. She keeps shaking her head. "Quinn, Quinn, Quinn. I can't handle this right now."

She takes her apron off in one swift movement. It drops

to the floor as she rushes out of the room, her fuzzy pink socks slip-sliding across the floor. I hear the creak of the stairs and then the soft click of her bedroom door shutting.

I bury my face in my hands, but the tears find a way to swim through the cracks. The kitchen feels bigger and lonelier than ever. I open the utensil drawer and grab a fork. I pick the pie closest to me and stab at it, scooping up a big bite.

The blackberry filling tastes like ash in my mouth. I spit it out in the sink. I wipe my mouth with the back of my hand.

Taking deep breaths, I steady myself against the kitchen island. I grab the teakettle off the stove and fill it up with water. I turn the knob that I've been told for years not to turn without a grown-up present. *Click, click, click*—a flame bursts to life underneath the burner.

I place the teakettle down and wait for it to scream.

TWENTY-THREE
CORA

Today only Dad is waiting for me in the hall when I get out of my appointment.

When I asked him why Grams didn't come, he told me he wanted some one-on-one time with me. On the drive to Dr. Randall's office, my stomach knotted and I wondered if he was going to ask me about all the time I've been spending with Quinn, but he didn't.

We rode in silence, listening to news on the radio. Dad turned the channel when they started talking about a shooting that had happened at a mall in North Carolina. He didn't look at me, just pressed the buttons on the steering wheel and the radio switched to Top 40 hits. I almost said something, but by the time I got up the courage, we were parked in front of the strip mall.

"Hey, kiddo," he says as I walk out of Dr. Randall's office. Dad hands me my corduroy jacket. It feels strange to call it mine when it used to be Mabel's. It's light brown and patterned with faint white flowers. It's big on me, but I started wearing it a few days ago when the weather turned colder.

I slide the jacket on and follow Dad back to the car.

"How about tonight we go somewhere else for dinner?"

I was really looking forward to egg rolls, but I say, "Sure."

Dad keeps the radio on the Top 40 station as he drives. It's pretty funny to watch my dad with his thick round-framed glasses and tweed blazer listening to a song about partying on the beach.

"Do you like this music?"

"Huh?" he says.

"This song. Why are we listening to it?"

He gives me a sheepish look. "Oh. Sorry. I don't know."

"You don't have to protect me, you know?"

His sheepish look deepens.

"From the news," I go on. "You didn't have to change it before."

His eyes look sad. "I changed it more for me than for you."

I don't press the subject. I lean back in my seat and try to enjoy the next song, which is also about partying. I wonder if these are the things Mabel was talking about when she said, "You just don't get it."

He parks the car in another strip mall. The main street

area of Chestnut is cute, but outside of that we're surrounded by lots of parking lots and strip malls.

I follow him as he walks toward a plain-looking restaurant called Aladdin's. The name is written in golden cursive script, and inside the window, I see booths that are decorated with bright red vases filled with plastic flowers.

"I was craving shawarma. What do you think?" He's wearing the same sheepish expression that he had on earlier in the car.

"Shawarma sounds good," I say as Dad pulls open the door to the restaurant.

He greets the man behind the counter in Arabic. I only know a few words in Arabic—like *marhaba* ("hello") and *shukran* ("thank you") and *inshallah* ("God willing," but when Dad says it, he usually means "I hope"). It seems like there should be a rule that if you are 50 percent of something, you should have to know at least 50 words.

"Yussef," Dad says. "This is my daughter, Cora. Cora, meet Yussef." Dad smiles and puts his arm around me, squeezing my shoulder. "I come here a lot for lunch."

"You do?" I ask.

"It's near campus."

And I guess it is. It's so strange to think of my dad getting lunch by himself. It's like you know your parents have lives outside of when you see them, but it's still totally bizarre to think about it.

Dad makes one of his nerdy finger-pointing motions

and I relax a little. I might not feel fully comfortable in my Middle Eastern–ness, but I feel very secure in my nerdiness. "Yussef's got the best shawarma in town." He turns to the counter to order. "Two sandwiches, please. And extra tahini sauce for me."

"Me too," I say, but only because Dad said it.

Yussef rings us up, and we take a seat in one of the booths.

"So," Dad says slowly. He runs his tongue over his top lip, which is one of his nervous tells.

"What is it?" I say.

"Straight shooter, I like that." It only takes Dad a minute to realize what he's said before he winces. Before Mabel's death, I never thought about how many everyday American phrases have to do with guns or shooting. They are so common in fact that even Dad, someone who didn't grow up here, has picked them up.

"Sorry," he mumbles.

"It's okay."

Our food arrives and Dad eagerly starts eating his sandwich. I stare at mine. "What were you going to say before?" I ask.

"Oh," Dad says. He dabs the corner of his mouth with a napkin.

"Um. Grams mentioned that . . ." He looks down at his sandwich. My dad is great at talking about cell growth, but when it comes to talking about uncomfortable personal family things, he tends to get a little bit lost.

"Grams, well, she told me . . ." Dad tries again.

I take a small sip of my Coke. The can sweats in my hand. "She told you I've been hanging out with Quinn again."

"Yes," he said.

We look at each other for a moment.

"Hey, Dad?"

"Yeah?"

"Why didn't you take Mabel and me to places like this more?"

His brow furrows. "What do you mean?"

"Like Middle Eastern restaurants. And Middle Eastern places."

He laughs and my face heats up. I sink into the comfy cushion of the booth.

"Middle Eastern places? You wish I'd taken you to eat more shawarma sandwiches?"

"Not exactly. But yes. I wish you'd taught me how to be Middle Eastern." What I don't say is: I wish you'd also taught Mabel. I wish she'd gotten the chance before she died.

"Honey, there's no one way to be Arab." He laughs again, and I feel totally stupid. I stare down at the table.

"What I mean is you know how to speak Arabic. And you know things about the culture. And I, like, well, I don't know anything." I tug at one of my curls. "The only thing

I have is that people think I look like I should know those things."

He gives me a sympathetic glance. "I didn't realize you were so curious about these things." He unscrews the cap of his water bottle. "I guess I always wanted you to feel like you belonged here. Especially because of . . ."

"Because of Mom leaving?"

"Yeah. I wanted you to feel and your sister to feel like Americans."

"But can't we be Arab and American? Like you."

He smiles. "You're right. You can." He balls a napkin up in his hand. "And that was my mistake for thinking that you couldn't. So what do you want to know?"

"Mabel and I wanted to know everything."

His eyes go cloudy. "I'm really sorry, Cora. I didn't know your sister had those questions . . ." His voice drifts off.

I hang my head. "It's okay, Dad. I'm not saying that to make you feel bad."

"Oh, I know, kiddo. But, hey, at least I can make it up to you, right? That has to be something."

I stare down at my half-eaten sandwich. I promise myself that once I've found the wormhole and saved Mabel, I'm going to make Dad answer all our questions. My sister and I will both get our answers.

"Hey, Corrie?"

I look up at him. "What?"

"Was this all a distraction technique to not have to talk about you hanging out with Quinn again?"

I shrug and pick at my sandwich, pinching the pita bread with my fingers. "Maybe a little. But I do really want to know things about being Arab."

"Okay. I promise I'll start to tell you more things about Lebanon and your family there, but I need you to talk to me about Quinn."

I'm scared to look at his face and find disappointment. Using the trick that Mabel once taught me, I keep my eyes glued to the space between his eyebrows. "Are you mad that I'm hanging out with her?"

"No! Definitely not!" The register of his voice makes me jump a little.

He reaches out to grab my hand. "Cora, kiddo, I'm so happy you're hanging out with Quinn again. I think that's very important."

My grip is weak, but I don't pull away from his touch. "Are you sure? Don't you blame Quinn at all for what . . . happened?"

Dad shakes his head. "Absolutely not." ·

He answers with so much certainty that, for a moment, I think that it's okay that I'm friends with Quinn again. That it's not a profound betrayal of Mabel. But then I quickly remind myself that I'm not really friends with Quinn again. I'm only working with her to save Mabel.

And then we can be friends again, of course. But we aren't friends again yet. Though that seems even harder to explain to Dad than my time-travel plot.

"You deserve stability. You've been through so much. Quinn has always been your best friend—"

"You don't blame any of the McCauleys? Not even Quinn's dad? The guns . . ." I can't say the words.

When Mabel first died, Grams and Dad sat me down. They told me they didn't want me to blame Quinn, but they also didn't feel comfortable with me going over to Quinn's house. At least for a little while. I told them they didn't have to worry about that because Quinn and I were never going to be friends again.

Dad's face drains of color. "Kiddo, you can't hold Quinn responsible for her parents."

"It's her family," I argue. "That's her dad. Parker was her brother."

Sometimes I worry that my grief is more anger than sadness—that the thing that I'm able to feel the most is this boiling-hot rage. It's the part that always feels the realest.

I feel like I can do something with it.

The sadness is useless. It's like wet socks. Anger is like walking through a fire. At least anger forces you to move.

"I can't forgive any of them," I say, and push my food away.

"Have you gone over to her house?" Dad asks.

I shake my head. "You told me not to."

Dad takes a deep breath. "I think for now that's still best. But I want you and Quinn to stay friends. Your friendship is important."

"We aren't really friends again. Not really," I mumble.

"But I thought you and Quinn were hanging out again?" Dad keeps putting extra emphasis on the words *hanging out*. It's clearly a phrase he picked up from Grams.

"It's hard to explain."

"You mean it's complicated?" Dad wriggles his eyebrows at me.

Dad knows I hate when people say *It's complicated*. I've never understood what that means. To me, it seems like complicated things are only things you haven't solved yet. A math equation—solve for x. A particularly tough spelling word—make a mnemonic device.

"Complicated," I repeat, giving him a funny look. "Will you teach me how to say that in Arabic?"

He grins and scratches the top of his head. "Sure thing, kiddo. Let me think about that."

After a few minutes of watching my dad make his signature thinking face, he says, "Probably the closest and best word would be *moaqqad*."

"*Moaqqad*," I repeat, and I can hear my pronunciation is a little off, but it's okay. It's another Arabic word. I'm getting closer to fifty.

TWENTY-FOUR
QUINN

Dear Parker,

When I first found out what you did, I thought I was going to split in two. I'd never felt pain like that in my life. I thought I would never be able to get out of bed again. I pulled the comforter over my head and wanted to disappear.

I didn't disappear. And I did get out of bed. But the pain has never gone away. Every time I think about you and what you did, I want to cry, but I try not to let myself. The pain goes away a little when I cry. And I know I deserve to feel the hurt.

I hope that maybe when I finally step through that wormhole and see you, this feeling will go away. Maybe I won't need to hurt anymore.

Sometimes I look at that picture of us at the beach

174

at Papa and Gammie's house in North Carolina. I don't recognize you, but I don't recognize me either. I don't think I know how to smile like that anymore.

I want to, though. I really want to.

Your sister,
Quinn

I meet up with Cora in the library after school. She has Quiz Bowl practice today, but she has thirty minutes before it starts.

"Hey," she says when she finds me at the back table. She drops her backpack down on the floor and slides into the seat next to me. "Look at this."

She pulls out her phone and presses play on a video. I sit up and lean in. I'm expecting it to have to do with wormholes, but it's a funny video of a dog jumping into a pool. Cora laughs when the dog splashes into the water.

I keep staring at the phone screen.

"What?" she says. "Don't you think it's cute?"

I open my mouth. "I—" But then I stop myself.

Cora understands what I was trying to say. "I have a lot of videos about time travel, too, but I just needed a quick break."

I want to say that I get that, but I'm not sure if I'm allowed to get that. I stare down at the wood grain of the library table.

"The dog was so cute, right?"

"Yeah." I smile a little.

"Let's watch it again."

She presses play, and we both laugh this time. It feels good to laugh with her. When the video is over, she slides her phone back into her pocket.

"I really think it's going to work, Quinn."

She doesn't say what the "it" is. She doesn't have to. The truth about what I knew about Parker turns inside of me, making me feel sick. I want to go back to how I felt a second ago, when we were laughing.

I want to forget about all of it again.

She stands up. "Practice time." She starts to go, but then turns around again. "Hey, do you want this?"

She digs in her backpack and pulls out a paper bag. She hands it to me. I look inside and see a blueberry muffin.

"Grams made it. Blueberry's still your favorite, right?"

I give her smile even though my insides still feel uneasy. "Thanks."

She waves and then heads to Quiz Bowl practice. I stay in the library for a little bit before I head home. I eat the muffin on my walk. It tastes so good. It tastes like love. But I know I don't deserve it.

When I get home, Dad's sitting on the couch. I'm surprised he's home from work already.

"Hey, Q," he says, and turns off the TV. "Where were you?"

"School."

He looks at his big golden wristwatch. "Didn't school let out a while ago?"

I swallow. "I was with Cora."

"Cora." He cups his chin with his hand and gives me a look. "Do you really think that's such a good idea?"

"She—she—" My brain is doing one of its Freeze-Ups.

Dad doesn't wait for me to get out my words. "Just be smart, Q. We can't afford any more mistakes."

I want to ask him about his guns and if he thinks that was a mistake. I want to ask him if he thinks it was a mistake not to talk to Parker more. To challenge him when he said hateful things at the dinner table. To make him come out of his room.

But my brain is like a giant glacier. It won't melt. I can't get a single word out of my mouth.

Dad sighs and leans farther back on the couch, his long legs stretching out in front of him. "I'm going to try to get your mom to look at this house in Turner's Point. I think it would be good for all of us. You could make new friends. Leave this all behind. Wouldn't that be great?"

"I—I—"

Dad answers for me again. "I just want you to be happy. I hope you know that." He clicks back on the TV. The sound of a sportscaster fills the house.

I stand there and watch the TV. Eventually Dad turns

177

around and looks at me. "I love you, Q. You didn't do anything wrong, okay?"

I want to scream, but I open my mouth and nothing comes out. Blood rushes to my face. I dig my fingernails into the flesh of my hands.

"Dad—" I did do something wrong. I saw Parker with the guns. I knew. "Dad, I—I—I—" I try again to tell him, but I can't make the words come out.

"It's okay. I know it's hard to talk about." He looks back at the TV. I wait for a while, but he doesn't turn around again.

I walk upstairs. Cupcake is curled up right next to Parker's door. I scoop her up and hug her to my chest. She purrs. My bottom lip trembles, but I don't let myself cry.

TWENTY-FIVE
CORA

I get to Coach Pearlman's room a little early. Owen is already there, though. He has his earbuds in. When I sit down, he takes one of them out.

"Hey. Listen to this." He hands me the earbud.

I put it in and hear a loud crash of drums and squealing guitars. Or I think they're guitars. I don't know that much about music, but I never like to admit that to Owen.

"What do you think?" he asks.

I knit my eyebrows together. "I don't know. It's kind of loud."

Owen laughs. "But that's the point."

I shrug, but find myself smiling. "I guess."

"Hm." He frowns a little and looks down at his phone. I worry I've totally said the wrong thing, but then he looks up at me and smiles. "I'm going to find a song you'll really like. Just wait."

"Okay." I smile even wider.

Mia rushes in right before practice starts. "What'd I miss?" she says.

"Owen's song."

She looks at me and then at Owen. "What?"

"Nothing," I say, but Owen and I exchange another smile. My stomach is all fizzy again, but this time, it doesn't bother me.

Coach Pearlman starts practice by laying out our chances of making the regional playoffs. It doesn't look great, but he's trying to motivate us that if we have a really strong match against Liberty Terrace Middle School, we'll still have a shot.

"So on that note, I've made a list of practice questions that reflect our biggest areas of weakness. I want to run through them."

He divides us up to scrimmage. Like usual, it's seventh graders versus eighth graders. Peter Tolbin starts out by getting three questions right in a row. He and Molly high-five while Mia and I exchange a frustrated look. Owen looks more nervous than frustrated.

"Come on," Mia says. "We have to at least get one."

And we do get one. The next question is about bees and I get it right. And the one after that is a math equation that I'm able to solve before Peter or Molly. Before I know it, I'm on a roll.

I keep reaching for the buzzer and getting the answers right.

"Good job, Hamed," Coach Pearlman says before he gives us a short break.

"Seriously," Mia says. "Good job. You're on fire today."

I grin. "Thanks."

Mia looks at me. "You seem different. Or, I mean you seem regular. Like the old you is back."

I shrug. "I'm able to focus today."

What I don't say is that I'm this close to saving to my sister—that I'm about to find a wormhole and change everything.

"Well, I like Cora," Mia says.

"Me too."

"Hey," Owen says. He hands me an earbud again. "Listen to this."

I put it in and hear a softer melody. I think it's a piano, but I'm not sure. Whoever is singing has a silky voice. I bob my head along.

"You like it?" Owen says.

I nod. "Yeah. It's nice."

He pumps his fist in the air. "See! I knew I would find your song."

I smile. I can't wait to tell Mabel about the song. I can't wait to tell Mabel about everything.

TWENTY-SIX
QUINN

Dear Parker,

I miss kicking the soccer ball around with you. I miss when Dad would join us, too.

Dad says our family can't afford to make any more mistakes.

I think we've already made too many mistakes.

And I'm worried it's a mistake to miss you. But I can't help it.

Your sister,
Quinn

"Wow. That looks so good."

It takes me a second to realize Ainsley is talking to me.

She leans over to get a better look at the acorn I'm shading. I'm putting the finishing touches on one of the banners for the fall festival.

"Oh," I say. "Thanks." My pencil hovers above the paper. I don't find it comfortable to draw when other people are watching me—it's like getting dressed in front of someone.

But Ainsley keeps staring at the banner. Her black hair is held back with a light pink headband today. It's not Wednesday, so she isn't in her soccer uniform, but she's wearing her team hoodie, which is almost as painful to see. The team hoodies are a dark navy color, and they look like they're made of extra-soft fabric. I imagine how great it would feel to wear one, to show off that I belonged to the team, that I belonged somewhere, anywhere.

"We could sure use you on the team," Ainsley says.

My jaw goes slack. *Did she just read my mind?* "Wh-what?" I stammer. I press my pencil point hard against the paper of the banner. It makes a dark smudge that I'll have to fix later.

"You're an awesome sweeper. We're kind of—" She stops talking for a minute to look over her shoulder at Scarlett. Determining it's safe, she keeps talking. "Weak right now at midfield. I'm doing the best I can, but it's hard when no one will pass the ball."

I give her a smile "I'm sure people pass."

"Oh, they do!" She makes a twitchy motion with her hands. "I didn't mean to talk trash, it's just that I miss playing with you."

The big smudge on the acorn doesn't seem so bad anymore. "Thanks, Ainsley."

"No problem. That's all I wanted to say. I really think you should've tried out."

I take a deep breath. "Maybe next year."

Scarlett walks over to us. She's holding a pair of scissors. "Found them," she says to Ainsley, making a direct point of not acknowledging me at all, which makes it super-glaringly obvious that the wormhole is really going to have to change things if there's going to be any chance of me trying out next year. In my head, I draw myself in the uniform, the navy knee socks over my shin guards, my hair in some elaborate braid that Scarlett's mom did.

"You look like you're thinking about something really delicious," Mrs. Euclid says. She puts her finger to her lips. Today she's wearing a bright pink lipstick and a neon-orange shirt with white polka dots. Her hair is pulled up in a high braided bun. "Hm. Let me guess. How delicious the apple cider at the fall festival is going to be?"

I twirl the pencil between my fingers and force myself to politely smile. "I don't think I'm going to go."

"What? You have to go. Plus, aren't you going to help hang up your work?" She gives me a big grin. "You've done such a good job, Quinn. You deserve to see your art on display."

"I've mostly just drawn acorns and pumpkins," I mutter.

She taps her finger against the acorn, avoiding the big smudge. "But what beautiful acorns and pumpkins they are. You're definitely going to come, right?"

"I'm—I'm—I'm—" I know the words I want to say, but I can't get them out. That's the worst part about The Freezing. The frustration of it. I wish my brain and my mouth would get it together.

"Hey," Mrs. Euclid says gently. "Can you come with me to my office? I need help with something."

I glance around at my classmates. To my relief, none of them are looking at me.

"It's okay," Mrs. Euclid says, like she knows what I'm thinking. "They're all busy."

I trail Mrs. Euclid back to her office. It's a small room off the library and it's anything but organized. I wonder if Cora has ever been inside here. She'd definitely freak out about the mess. But I kind of like it. All the books waiting to be cataloged, the multicolored Post-it Notes, and the coffee mugs holding various pencils and pens. The mess makes the room feel like a place where exciting things are happening. It makes the room feel alive.

Mrs. Euclid lifts a stack of books off her desk chair and motions for me to take a seat. I sit down and she perches on the desk, pushing back against a big pile of papers.

"So," she says. "What's going on?"

My eyes wander around the office. They land on a *Star Wars* poster. It's attached to the wall with glittery blue thumbtacks. "Nothing's going on."

"But you don't want to go to the fall festival."

I shrink into my chair. "It's not really my thing."

"You were there last year."

I look up in surprise. I didn't really know Mrs. Euclid at this point last year. That was before it happened, before I started coming to the library to hide out. Before I had a reason to hide out.

She seems to register my surprise, so she expands on that thought, "You and Cora had matching costumes. They were so cute."

"Yeah. I was mustard and she was ketchup." Grams made the costumes for us. Cora had it in her head that she really wanted to be condiments for some reason. I can't remember the reasoning now, which, to be honest, makes me feel a little bad.

"That's right!" Mrs. Euclid claps her hands together. "So what gives?"

I give her a look. She can't really be asking me that question.

"You—you—you know," I say. I go back to staring at the *Star Wars* poster and trace the outline of Yoda in my head.

Mrs. Euclid takes a step closer to me. She kneels down so she's close to eye level with me, but I still don't look at her. "Quinn, if I'm off base, you should definitely feel free to ask me to stop talking, but does this have something to do with your brother?"

Hearing the word *brother* come out of her mouth makes me shiver. Mrs. Euclid and I have never once talked about Parker. "Uh, yeah," I say stiffly.

"Quinn," she says slowly, "I want you to listen to me. You can't spend your life atoning for what your brother did. Do you know what I mean by atoning?"

The truthful answer is that I'm only about 10 percent sure that I do, but I'm not about to admit that. "I'm not dumb, you know."

Mrs. Euclid bends her head toward me. "Oh, Quinn, I know. You are so smart. You're one of the most talented students I've had in a long time. Your drawings are very detailed. You have such a great eye, which is always a sign of a brilliant mind."

I know she's trying to be nice, but for some reason there's an eruption happening at my core. It's that lava-spitting feeling again. My anger, the anger I've tried so hard to ignore for so long, is bubbling up. "You don't have to compliment me. I'm not, like, a sad dog."

She's the first teacher who has ever told me that I'm smart. I don't know what to do with that. I don't deserve those nice words.

There's a long stretch of silence. When I look up, I see a puddle of hurt on Mrs. Euclid's face. It only makes the anger inside of me bubble more.

"Look," I say, "you can tell me all you want that I shouldn't *atone*"—I say that word like it's a rubber band, stretching it out all the way in my mouth—"for what my brother did, but you don't know what you're talking about because what he did it's—it's—it's my fault. It's my—my— my fault."

I suck in a deep breath. The vacuuming of tears. I'm not going to cry. I can't. I won't.

The silence that ribbons through the air is so heavy, it's almost like there's another person in the small and crowded office. The ghostly silence drifts around the room as Mrs. Euclid visibly struggles with what to say next. I bet she's really regretting inviting me back into her office now. I look at the Yoda poster. I wish it would come alive and give me some wise advice.

"I understand that you might feel guilt, Quinn, and that's normal. Have you talked with someone?" Mrs. Euclid finally says.

"Yeah, right. Who is there to talk to?"

"Ideally I'd love for you to have the opportunity to talk with a professional."

I keep staring at Yoda and tracing him in my mind. His ears are the most difficult part. I wonder how long the artist spent on them. I don't bother to answer Mrs. Euclid. I can't. How do I tell her that I don't come from the type of family that's going to let me talk to a professional? That professionals are only for kids like Cora. For kids who deserve help.

"Quinn, please look at me."

My eyes feel as heavy as stones. I can barely lift them up. But when I do, I see Mrs. Euclid's face is like a window—clear and open. It's inviting me in. The thing about windows, though, is that they shatter easily.

I sink into the chair. "Believe me, you don't want me to talk about this with you."

"But I do."

I shake my head. "You think you do, but you don't."

"Try me."

The eruption happens. The angry hot lava pours out of me. I jump up from the chair. My whole body is shaking. "I saw him. I saw him open my dad's safe. I knew that he knew where the guns were. And I saw—" I pause, but not because I'm Freezing Up.

No.

This time I pause because I want to get my words just right. I want them to sting.

I want them to burn.

"I saw in his eyes that something bad was going to happen. And you know what I did?" I don't wait for her to answer. "I didn't do a thing. Not a single thing. I—"

The lava is cooling inside me. It's turning into something much more dangerous. Big, fat salty tears. I turn away from Mrs. Euclid. I can't let her see me cry.

"Oh, Quinn," Mrs. Euclid says quietly. "It wasn't your fault."

Her eyes well up. She stares at me, but she doesn't look like she's seeing a monster. I only see sympathy on her face. Sympathy that I don't deserve.

"Did you not hear what I said?" My voice is trembling. I'm struggling to hold on to my hot anger. "I saw him. I—I—I knew."

"I need you to listen to me, Quinn. And I mean really listen. What your brother did was not your fault. That responsibility isn't yours. I know you feel like you should've told someone, and probably you should've, but that doesn't mean that what happened is your fault. That's a burden that is not yours to bear. And it's much too heavy for you to be carrying around. Have you talked to your parents about this?"

I shake my head.

"Can I give you a hug?"

I surprise myself by nodding. Mrs. Euclid wraps me up in a tight embrace. A single tear slides down my cheek. I vacuum it up as fast as I can.

"It's not your fault, Quinn. Do you hear me? But I really think you need to talk to your parents."

"I ca-can't. They'll be mad. And they'll tell me I can't tell anyone because . . ."

Mrs. Euclid doesn't rush me. She keeps me in the hug. It makes me feel safer than I've felt in a really long time.

"Because," I say again once I find my words, "Cora and I, the two of us are trying to fix things. But I don't know if it's going to work because I haven't told Cora the truth . . ."

Mrs. Euclid pulls away from me so she can look me in the eyes. "Fix things? Quinn, I need you to listen to me again. None of what happened is your responsibility to fix it. It's my responsibility." She thumbs at her chest. "And it's the responsibility of other adults. We've created a world that is unsafe for you kids. And it's our job to stand up and figure out how to protect you."

When she finishes talking, I see that she's crying. That makes me want to cry harder. I can't stand to see my teacher crying.

"I have to tell Cora, don't I?" I whisper.

"It would probably make you feel better to tell Cora. But I think you definitely need to tell your parents, Quinn. And I really think it would help you to talk with someone. I could call your parents and give them some names if that would help?"

I shake my head.

"But you'll talk to them, right?"

I bite my lip. "I'll think about it."

There's a knock on the door of Mrs. Euclid's office. She gives me a look that lets me know both that it's okay to go, and that this probably won't be the last time we talk about this. I race back to the tables and pick back up my pencil. The acorn looks different than before.

How do you draw guilt? I wonder.

But swiftly another question comes to me. One that's even harder.

How do you draw forgiveness?

I imagine sketching it, aloe lotion on a sunburn, a grilled cheese on a snowy day, a soft sweatshirt that feels like a second skin.

But I can't quite figure it out so I go back to shading the acorn's top.

TWENTY-SEVEN
CORA

Here are the statistics:

Since me and Quinn's last attempt at time travel, I have:

Watched three documentaries
Read seventeen more scientific articles
Took four pages of notes
Played out at least fifteen different scenarios in my head

Which is all to say that I'm ready for today. Today is going to be The Day. It's going to be because it has to be. And also because I've done the homework and good things always happen when you do the homework. That's a solid fact.

I tighten my grip on my backpack. I've stuffed it full of some of Mabel's belongings. I'm nervous about bringing them outside, but it's the right thing to do. If it helps make the wormhole appear, it's worth it.

When I get to the tree, Quinn is already there. I watch her for a minute. She's pacing by the trunk of the tree, muttering something under her breath.

"Hey, you okay?" I call out.

"Yeah." Quinn spins around. Her white freckled skin is splotchy with pink from the cold air, and her red hair falls in a tangled mess around her face. She doesn't look okay at all.

"You sure?"

Quinn eyes my backpack. "You brought the stuff?"

I nod. "And did you?"

She points at a sad-looking plastic grocery bag. "I couldn't find much."

"Your parents threw out a lot of his things?"

She looks like she's about to say yes, but ends up shaking her head. "I, uh, I, didn't know what to bring."

I narrow my eyes. "I gave you specific instructions."

"I—I—I know. I just—" Her hands hang at her sides. "I'm sorry."

I walk over to the plastic bag. Inside there's a brass Little League trophy and a completely nondescript black notebook. I pick up the notebook. When I flip through it, I see that it's blank. "Was this important to him?"

Quinn shrugs.

"Why aren't you taking this seriously?"

"I am," she insists.

There's something going on with her. I know there is

because I can read her better than anyone. This reminds me of when her stomach hurt really bad on our second-grade field trip because the bus ride made her nauseous, and she didn't want to tell me because she was embarrassed. But I knew something was wrong and so I followed her into the bathroom and helped hold her hair while she puked into the toilet. I really hope this isn't another puking situation.

"Fine," I say, not wanting to get into it with her. I need to be positive. I wrote that over and over again in my notes. Almost every anecdote I read about someone finding a wormhole talked about the power of positivity. I know Dad would say that sounds like fake science, but still. At this point, I'm willing to stretch a little.

"Let's set up the barrier," I say. That's another thing I read about. It's supposed to help.

Without answering, Quinn begins collecting twigs. We work in silence, quietly creating a wide circle around the tree that's made of twigs and random stones that we find. Quinn even pulls a few wet rocks out of the creek.

Once the circle is finished, we stand inside it.

"Looks pretty good, don't you think?"

Quinn nods.

I study her face. "You sure you're okay?"

She pushes her hair behind her ears. "Yeah. I'm fine."

"Okay. Well, I think the barrier is going to help. It gives our experiment limits, you know? Scientific experiments need limits."

Quinn nods again.

Her silence scratches at me. Quinn is always quiet, but usually it's a comfortable silence. But right now it's like a buzzy static, like how the car stereo sounds when it gets stuck between radio stations.

"Well," I say slowly. "Let's unpack Mabel's and . . ." I can't say his name. I stare at Quinn's shoes.

She gets the message though because she goes and grabs the plastic bag. "Where do you want these?"

I carefully unpack Mabel's things. My hands tremble as I set down Waddle, her stuffed penguin, who she would tell you she stopped sleeping with when she was nine, but the truth was, he always had a spot right next to her pillow.

I don't want Waddle to get any dirt on him, so I gently lay out a washcloth I brought from home and put Waddle on top. Then I put Mabel's silver star necklace, a tube of dark plum lip gloss, and *The Tale of Despereaux*, which was her all-time favorite book, down next to Waddle.

Mabel was so much more than these objects, but these objects also say Mabel. I hope the wormhole agrees.

"You can put his things over there." I point to a spot that's close to where I set up Mabel's things, but not too close.

"We don't have anything from the others," I say quietly.

"I'm sure it's okay," Quinn says. "This looks really good, Cora."

I smile a little. It's a cold day, but sunlight is filtering down from the sky. The stones and the twigs we've laid out glitter in the sun.

I clasp my hands together. "I think it's going to work today."

"I hope so," Quinn says.

"Me too." I stare at the giant oak tree. "You really think the wormhole will look like a door?"

Quinn shuffles her feet. "I mean, I don't know. That's just how I imagine it."

I tilt my head. "Hm. I always envisioned it looking like a blurry hole. Does that make sense? Like an out-of-focus swirl in the middle of the tree."

None of the articles I read gave an exact description of what the wormhole looked like, which I frankly found to be maddening. It would help if I knew exactly what I was looking for.

Quinn raises her eyebrows. "Sort of?"

"I guess I could try to picture a door." I stare harder at the giant oak tree. I'm willing to picture anything if it will bring me to Mabel. I can feel my eyeballs starting to water from holding them open so long without blinking.

Quinn stays silent. When I glance over at her, she's not even looking at the tree. She's staring at Waddle. My stomach pinches.

"So," I say. "Let's try again?"

Quinn turns from Waddle to me. "Okay."

I point at Waddle. "You remember him?"

She nods. Her lips move like she might say something else, but she doesn't.

"I miss her so much, Quinn." I can hear my voice breaking and I step closer to the giant oak tree. It feels good to lean against it. It's steady. It can hold the weight of everything.

Quinn stares at her shoes. "I know you do."

Before I realize what I'm doing, I've walked over to Quinn. I hug her tightly. My eyes are blurry with tears. "And I've missed you so much, too. I don't know if I've told you that yet."

She jumps a little in surprise, but she hugs me back. It feels even steadier than leaning against the giant oak tree. It reminds me of when we did a three-legged race together when we were kids and it felt so easy to become one person. I want to feel whole like that again.

Quinn starts to trace a heart on my back. We used to play this game all the time when we were little. One person draws a shape, and the other person tries to guess what it is.

"It's a heart," I whisper.

"Yup," she says.

I pull away from her. I grab a Kleenex out of my corduroy jacket and wipe my nose. "I think I might need your help climbing the tree again," I admit.

Quinn smiles for the first time all day. "No problem. Follow me."

She effortlessly hops up onto one of the lower branches. Once she's hoisted herself farther up, she bends down and stretches out her hand. "Here."

I take her hand and follow her up.

TWENTY-EIGHT

QUINN

Dear Parker,

You know how in comic book movies, they always give the villain this elaborate backstory? I mean, you can see that the Joker is going to end up a bad guy from like a million miles away. It's so obvious.

But I don't think that's how it is in real life.

I wish I would have seen it.

Or maybe the problem is that I did see it, but I didn't understand.

I understand now. And I really hope it's not too late.

Your sister,
Quinn

Cora and I sit back-to-back, our shoulders slowly rising with each shallow breath. I wonder how many times Cora and I have sat like this over the course of our lives. One hundred? Two hundred? I don't know. I can't help thinking that this might be the last time.

A few weeks ago, Mrs. Euclid told our class that art is as much about remembering as it is about seeing. I mentally draw us like this so I can remember it, so I can have this memory forever.

"Ready?" Cora asks. "Let's start."

I squeeze my eyes shut. *The science classroom*, I tell my brain. I hold the image. The lab tables and their steel sinks. I even get as far as imagining Parker's dark boots on the tiled classroom floor, but then I'm back in the upstairs hallway of my house, following him into my parents' room.

I try to reach out for my brother's shoulder, but my hand slides right through his shoulder blade.

He's not real.

None of this is real.

My eyes snap open and I can't concentrate any longer. But Cora's breathing is still steady. I know she's doing the best she can to picture that morning. She's trying.

It's me. I'm the problem.

I look up. The sky overhead is a deep-blue color—the type of sky you see drawn with thick acrylic paints, all texture and swirls. The sun is slipping down to the ground, leaving a trail of eggy light. All of it looks close enough to touch. I reach my hand out but feel only air. Another illusion.

"It didn't work," Cora whispers. "We're still here."

I have to tell her. I know that I do, but I also don't know how I possibly can.

"Core—" I start.

"What?" She shuffles on the branch, flipping herself around. I do the same.

"What do you think we're missing?" she asks. "I need to check something in my notebook."

"Core—" I try again, but she's already crawling down. I'm impressed with how quickly she's hopping from branch to branch. She remembers the path down from before.

When she's almost to the forest ground, she turns to look up at me. "Are you coming?"

The ground looks so far away. For a moment, I'm six years old again, and I'm staring down at Parker, begging him to help me get down. I can see his younger face, the worry in his eyes, the smatter of freckles on his nose. I shove that image away.

My brother is gone. And I have to get out of the tree myself.

When my feet reach the ground, I'm still thinking about my brother. His face is rotating through my mind, a kaleidoscope of him at different ages. The more I try to see him clearly, to really hold an image of him, the hazier he becomes. The more he seems like he was always a stranger.

Cora is buried in her notebook. She's frantically flipping the pages, searching for an answer that I know she won't find.

"Core," I say, my voice quivering.

"What?" she says, not looking up. "I have to be missing something. I just don't get what it is. Do you think we need to say something before we start the visualization? A formula or equation or something?" She flips to another page.

"I—" I start, but my mouth feels like it's filled up with cement. "I—I—I have to t-tell you something."

"Okay. Tell me." She doesn't even look up. She keeps flipping.

"I saw him."

"Who?"

"Parker."

At the mention of his name, Cora looks up. "What do you mean you saw him? Do you mean just now? Did the visualization actually work?"

The hope I see in her eyes cracks me open. I feel so guilty that I can't stand it.

"I—I—" I search for the words. I back up so that I can press my spine against the giant oak tree. My giant oak tree. This tree that I really believed would make everything okay again.

Cora blinks at me. I don't bother to blink back. I'm not okay. Nothing about what I'm about to say is okay.

"Quinn?" she prompts. She sets the notebook down and takes a step toward me. I put up my hand to stop her.

"I saw him, Core. I saw him open my dad's safe. Not the day it happened, before. A few weeks before. But I knew—"

I don't tell her about how narrow the hallway suddenly seemed, like a tunnel that was tightening around me. How I held my breath so tight that I felt like I couldn't breathe. How he picked up one of the guns and turned it over, cradling it in his hands like he was impressed with the weight of it.

I don't tell her about the look in his eyes when he turned around and saw me. How it was so vacant at first, like he was staring at a ghost instead of his own sister. And how the vacant look slowly turned to a glare and he yelled at me to go away, but I didn't move, not even an inch. I stayed and kept holding my breath. I don't tell her how relieved I'd felt when I watched him put the gun back in the safe.

The exhale I'd finally let out. How stupid I'd been to think that was the end when really it was the beginning.

I know I should've said something then.

I just didn't have the words.

And I don't have the words now.

Cora's eyes slowly move into slits. I brace myself.

But she doesn't say anything.

There is only a stony silence.

I try to meet her eyes, but I'm not brave enough. I stare at a pile of fallen leaves. "I didn't know what he was going to do, Core. I really didn't."

Cora takes a few steps back from me. She stumbles over a stray branch, catching her balance at the last moment. "But you knew. You saw him. And you didn't do anything."

The sky is getting darker. The sun has almost completely slipped behind the clouds. I hold my breath like I did that day in the hallway.

"And you didn't tell me. All this time. You didn't tell me," Cora continues. "You've lied to me and wasted our time. You knew this all along—"

"I didn't—"

"No," Cora says. "You didn't."

"Please, Cora. You have to understand—"

"I don't have to do anything!" Cora snaps. Her eyes are ringed with red, but she's not crying.

I'm not crying either. My whole body is frozen.

"You need to leave," Cora says quietly. "Right now."

"Please," I plead. "I want to help still. I want to make this right."

Cora balls her hands into fists and taps one against her forehead. "I was so wrong to trust you. Just leave, Quinn. Don't make this worse than it is."

"Cora, please," I beg. "But what about the plan?"

Cora crosses her arms over her chest. "I don't need your help. And I certainly don't want your help anymore." She throws me a hard stare. It's so piercing that I can feel it deep inside my chest. "Do you know why penguins can't fly?"

"What?"

"Do you know why penguins can't fly?" she repeats.

I shake my head. I don't understand why she's talking about penguins right now.

"Because there are no land predators in Antarctica. But in the Arctic, birds do fly because there are land predators. Like polar bears, for instance."

"Uh, okay," I say, not exactly following.

"It's critically important to understand your surroundings. I can't believe I trusted you. What a mistake that was."

I stare again at the dead leaves on the ground, a medley of burnt red and golden brown, a collection of fallen things. I can't cry. I won't let myself.

"Core—"

"Quinn. I want you to leave now."

"I—"

Cora gives me a withering look. It makes me feel like I've drunk one of those *Alice in Wonderland* shrinking potions. Suddenly, I am two inches tall, trembling and cowering on the ground.

"You don't get it, do you? I don't want you to be here. I don't want to ever even see you again. Do you understand?"

Her olive-brown face turns red, and she starts to shout: "GO! Just go. PLEASE GO."

As Cora shouts, I swear I can hear the sound of my own heart cracking—a sharp snap, right down the center.

I know I should stay. I should hold my ground. Because if I run away, I become the lying coward Cora thinks I am.

But I can't stand the way Cora is looking at me—a mix of disappointment and anger, like I'm the worst person in the whole world, like I'm a monster.

And I know that she's right.

I turn and run away. I run away from her, but really I wish I could run away from me. Once I'm out of sight, I finally let the tears stream down my face.

TWENTY-NINE
CORA

Dad finds me at the kitchen table. I came down for a snack, and I've been staring at the same page of my time-travel research notebook for what feels like a whole century. No matter how long I stare, I still can't figure out what I'm missing.

Wormhole. Exotic matter. Point A to point B.

My eyes begin to cross, and two more words sneak in: Quinn McCauley. I quickly push that thought away, though. I'm not going to waste time on Quinn's betrayal. I've wasted enough time on her.

I won't let myself be upset. I just won't. She's not worth it.

Good scientists do not let themselves get distracted by speed bumps. All experiments experience setbacks.

I've been dedicating all my time to this. I've skipped

Quiz Bowl practice, and I've even missed a couple of home-work assignments. But in the end, I know it will be worth it.

"What are you working on there, kiddo?" Dad sits across from me. He unwraps a granola bar and takes a big bite. Dad and I are both granola-bar people. Grams can't stand granola bars as a subspecies of snack, but I think Dad and I are on the right side of history when it comes to this particular preference. Science will someday prove us right.

I take the last bite of my granola bar and move my note-book away so he can't read my notes.

His eyebrows arch up. "Secret project?"

I shrug. "Not really."

He chews and gives me a toothy smile. "Well, I have something for you." He does a goofy dramatic twist and pulls out something from behind his back. It's a slender book. He slides it across the table to me.

I pick it up and read the cover. The book is called *The Prophet*. It's by a guy named Kahlil Gibran. I flip the book over. "What is this?"

"A book of poetry."

I wrinkle my nose. "Poetry?"

Dad and I are not poetry people. I don't think Grams is, but I don't really know. She might be. Generally speaking, she has a higher tolerance for that type of thing.

"Kahlil Gibran is Lebanese. This was one of my favorite books when I was growing up."

"*You* liked a book of poems?"

Dad laughs. "This is a very famous book, Cora. And Gibran has a lot of wise things to say about life and love—" Dad pauses. He taps the bridge of his glasses. "And loss."

"Oh," I say quietly. I stare at the black-and-white photograph of the author. "Kahlil Gibran? Am I saying that right?"

"Kah-LEEL ji-BRAHN," Dad helps to guide me.

I mimic his pronunciation.

"Perfect."

I let out a whistle of pride and flip through a few pages of the book. "I guess I can check it out, but I don't know how much I'll understand. I don't really get poetry."

I hear Mabel's voice in my head, *You wouldn't get it. You don't get it.* I frown.

Dad puts his hands up and turns out his palms. "No pressure. I just thought—" He looks at the book with longing. "Well, the other day you asked me about Lebanon. And this is a book I read when I was young. So I thought I would share it with you."

My stomach feels mushy. Mabel used to call it the mashed potato feeling. We'd both get it whenever Dad got like this. I give him the biggest smile I can muster. "Thanks, Dad. Really. It's great."

His eyes light up. "Really?"

"Really. I promise I'll read it."

"You know, kiddo, poetry and science aren't that different."

I pucker my lips with doubt.

"They're both trying to solve the mysteries of our universe," Dad explains. He reaches across the table to tap the cover of the book. "Sometimes reading a poem can give you a different perspective on a scientific concept. It can make your brain work in a different way."

I glance from the book to my notebook. I take a deep breath. This is my chance. I know I have to take it. "Hey, Dad?"

"Yeah?"

"Does Gibran talk about time travel?"

Dad scratches the back of his neck. "Hm. I don't think so. But—" Dad holds up a finger, telling me to wait while his brain processes. I give him a patient nod. "He does talk about time. Can I see that?"

I hand the book to him. He turns the pages.

"'You would measure time the measureless and the immeasurable,'" Dad reads aloud.

I wrinkle my nose again. "And what does that mean?"

Dad laughs. "I'm not quite sure. I think it means that time is fluid. That it isn't quantifiable. At least not in the way that we perceive it to be. We've given time a linear order because it suits us. But the order we've given it is actually an illusion. That's not really how time operates."

My heartbeat quickens. "And isn't that the theory behind time travel?"

Dad's forehead creases with thought. "Yes. The idea is

that time isn't linear in the way that we experience it. That it's more of a circular thing. Well, that's one of the theories anyway." The creases on his forehead deepen. "Why are you so interested in time travel?"

I put my hand over my notebook. A protective instinct. "No reason. I just find it fascinating. Don't you?"

Dad nods quickly. "Definitely."

I gather the nerve to ask the question that's burning inside of me. "Do you think it's possible? Time travel?"

Dad tilts his head back and forth. He sometimes becomes a bobblehead when he's deep in thought. "Yes. Theoretically."

"A scientist at MIT said he thinks it's likely a human has already done it."

Dad gives me a wry smile. "I see you've done your homework."

I keep my palm pressed against my notebook and shrug. "I've read some articles."

"You know . . ." Dad trails off.

"What?"

He has a faraway look in his eyes. "Your mother once said something rather poetic to me about time."

Your mother. The words make me sit up straight in my chair. "Mom was into poetry?"

"No," Dad says, laughing again. He runs his hand through his dark curls, which are beginning to gray at the edges. "She was of a similar opinion to you on the subject."

I squirm. I'm not sure how I'm supposed to feel about that.

"We were discussing the shape of time," Dad says.

"The shape of time?"

"Yeah. The idea that time is circular. Or at least not the straight line that we often conceive of it to be." He makes a circular motion with his finger.

"And Mom didn't think time was circular?"

"Well," he says, and his eyes get that distant look again. As I watch his face, I wonder if he's time-traveling right in front of me. If he's going back to his college days, when he first met my mom. "We were talking about time travel and your mother said, 'I think the answer lies in figuring out the shape of time. And the shape of time is probably like the shape of thunder. We think it's impossible to map, but that's because we haven't pushed our brains to think in that way.'"

Dad claps his hands in front of him. He's smiling, but not at me. Catching himself, he shakes his head and gives me a bashful look. "Anyway, I thought that was a neat thing to say. It's stuck with me. Your mother had a brilliant mind. She saw the world differently than other people." He tips his head toward me. "Much like you, kiddo."

"The shape of thunder," I repeat. I reach for my notebook, and I scribble the quote. I put asterisks around it, which is what I do whenever I'm taking notes in class and my teacher emphasizes a fact so much that it's obvious it will be on the next quiz.

There's a faint ringing in my ears. *Thunder.* Perhaps this is the thing I've been missing.

The shape of thunder. What a strange phrase. It doesn't quite make sense. I would say it's an oxymoron, but it feels even bigger than that. It's more than contradictory; it's impossible. A thing that doesn't actually exist, but possibly could. An impossible thing that could actually be possible.

Like finding a wormhole. Like time travel.

Dad points at my notebook. "You like that, huh?"

My heart is racing, but I'm trying to act cool. "It's a neat quote."

Dad gives me a knowing look. "I think so, too."

I clutch my notebook and the book of poems to my chest. "Dad?"

He startles from whatever thought he was having. "Hm?"

"Thank you for the book," I say. "And for the . . . story."

Dad grins wide enough that I can see his front two teeth that are crooked. Mabel used to love to tease him about them, but I've always liked the way they are. It's like I wouldn't have even known they weren't straight if it hadn't been pointed out.

And that's how I feel about Mom leaving. I want to tell Dad that, but I don't know how without sounding really strange. Or hurting his feelings about his teeth.

"You're a really good dad," I say, standing up from the table. "And Mabel thought so, too. What I'm trying to say is that I'm really glad you're my dad. Is that a silly thing to say?"

Dad turns his head away from me a little, but I can still see that his eyes are teary. "No, kiddo. That's a beautiful thing to say. And, hey, I'm really glad I'm your dad, too."

He stands up and walks around the table. Pulling me close, he kisses the top of my head. "We're going to be okay, Corrie. It's been tough, but I know we're going to be okay."

"I know," I whisper, staring down at that impossible but possible phrase. *The shape of thunder.*

THIRTY

QUINN

Dear Parker,

I told Cora about how I saw you with Dad's guns.
She hates me now. Like she should.

Mrs. Euclid told me that telling the truth would make
me feel lighter. But I still feel pretty heavy. I haven't
told Mom or Dad. I'm scared to.

I keep thinking about all the things I didn't know
about you. Like what you were doing, what you were
planning, when you sat alone in your room for hours.

I also think about the things I did know about you.
That you liked pickles. That your favorite color was
fire-engine red. That when you found something really
funny, you tipped your head back all the way with
laughter. I don't remember the last time I heard you
laugh.

It's probably important for me to remember things like that. But sometimes I don't want to.

I think I hate you. I just sometimes forget.

Your sister,
Quinn

Mom looks like she's ready to go to a party or something. Since it happened, she hardly wears anything other than leggings and cozy sweaters and her cooking apron, but she's standing in the foyer wearing crisp dark jeans and a billowy white blouse. Her hair is swept up neatly, and she's even wearing her "Leading Lady" lipstick.

"You really don't have to give me a ride," I say.

Mom is scrolling through something on her phone. "But, sweetheart, it looks like it's going to rain."

I imagine drawing a muzzle over my mouth, a clamp on my tongue. This whole past year, I've walked to and home from school no matter what the weather was. Last winter, I walked home one day when it was so cold I couldn't feel my toes by the time I got home.

"I'd be okay" is all I manage to mumble.

Mom looks at herself in the mirror. "It's okay. It's no problem. I've always loved the fall festival."

If eyes could stretch, mine would be touching their toes. "Are you going to co-co-come?"

She gives her own reflection a sad smile. "Oh, no. I'll just drop you off. But it will be nice to get a little peek at drop-off."

"You could come. I know it's mostly for kids, but some parents chaperone."

Mom touches my cheek. "Not this year."

We say bye to Dad. He tells us both that we look nice. This makes Mom smile wide and seeing that makes me so happy that for second I forget about all the reasons I have not to smile.

I follow Mom to the car. When I climb into the back seat, I realize it's been a long time since I've ridden in it. On the rare occasion that I leave the house with my parents, we take Dad's car.

The cloth seats smell like the floral deodorizer Mom has hanging from the dashboard, and there's still the faint Kool-Aid stain from when I was little and spilled my soccer snack. I look around for any signs of Parker, but I can't find a single one.

I'm not sure if that should make me feel happy or sad.

We drive in silence. When we reach the drop-off zone, Mom keeps her hands on the wheel. I watch her study the stream of kids that are pouring out of their cars. Lots of them are dressed in costume. Bea, my old tetherball buddy, walks by decked out in a tutu and fairy wings, and someone I don't recognize passes by in a pretty awesome dinosaur suit.

I'm wearing jeans and a basic long-sleeve T-shirt. I can't believe I'm actually here. The idea of putting together a costume seemed like way too big of a hurdle to clear, but now I'm wondering if I would feel safer hiding behind a mask or a wig.

"Mom—" I start.

We haven't talked about our fight last week. I mean, we've talked. But we haven't talked about it.

We never talk about it.

"Yes?" she says, but doesn't bother to look back at me.

"Do you think there's a way to f-f-f-fix things?"

At this, she turns around. Her bottom lip quivers. Her forehead is full of wrinkles, but she looks so young. I feel like I should hug her, keep her safe. "What?"

"Never mind." I stare at the Kool-Aid stain. I don't want to make her cry. Not today. "I'll see you later." I get out of the car and slam the door a little harder than I should.

I do my best to blend into the throng of kids. If people stare at me, I don't notice. They seem too busy checking out each other's costumes.

When I enter the gym, I find Mrs. Euclid standing on the second step of a small ladder. She jumps off it when she spots me.

"Quinn! You're here!" She gives my shoulder a squeeze. "Finally. We are very behind." She tosses her arms up like she's sprinkling confetti.

I glance around the gym. I see lots of kids from art class, including Scarlett and Ainsley. The banners we made are hanging on every wall, and all the different clubs and sports teams have set up stalls. I try not to stare too long at the girls' soccer team's booth. But it looks really nice. Ainsley must've spent a lot of extra time on their decorations.

My heart skips when I spot Quiz Bowl's stall. It's way in the back corner, and I can't see if Cora's there or not.

"Come on," Mrs. Euclid urges. "I'm trying to hang your banner. Right up front." She gives me a big smile. I know I should be proud that my art is what's going to greet people when they come in, but I'm not sure I do.

Really I'm not sure if I'm allowed to ever feel proud about anything ever again if I don't find the wormhole. I stare over my shoulder at the Quiz Bowl booth again.

Mrs. Euclid follows my eyes. "Looking for Cora?"

I don't answer. I tape one corner of the banner to the wall. Mrs. Euclid handles the other corner.

"Bravo," she says, admiring my work. "It looks great, Quinn. I'm so glad you came."

"Yeah," I say weakly, taking in the crowded gym again. Bass-filled music thumps in through speakers, which makes all the decorations flap like they're dancing. I study the welcome banner. The smudge near the top of the acorn is mostly gone. If you didn't know to look for it, you probably wouldn't know it had ever been there. But the shadow of that smudge of imperfection is all I can see.

All the costumes blend together. There are lots of superheroes and tons of girls dressed in white dresses with matching white unicorn headbands. The once-shiny wooden floor turns dusty with flecks of mud and stray dead leaves that have been dragged in from outside by all the foot traffic.

I try to picture my brother here when he was my age. My memory isn't very clear. Back then, I didn't think to pay much attention. I know he dressed up like a baseball player (a lazy throwaway costume that he came up with minutes before leaving the house with some help from Dad) and that he went with his friends Joe and Anderson. I wonder if when he stood in this gym, if he was already starting to think those horrible things. Or if on that night, he was just happy to be with his friends. If he stood awkwardly like everyone else, moving between the booths, swaying to the loud music.

I don't know. And I don't know if I want to.

I keep looking around. Maybe this is the place to find the wormhole. Squeezing my eyes shut, I sketch all the details of my brother's costume that I can remember—his baseball cap that covered his short dark hair, the jersey that hung down past his waist because it belonged to my dad, his white pants with navy stripes.

I imagine a swirling hole opening up right in front of me. Stepping into it, I'll travel back to that night. I'll talk to my brother. Twelve-year-old Parker will listen to me.

I mean, I think he would.

Maybe if I could just talk to him then, if only for ten

minutes, I would be able to change everything, and then when I stepped back through the wormhole I would be here, and everything would be the same, but also really different, because Parker wouldn't have hurt anyone. And Mabel and everyone else would still be alive, Cora and I would still be friends. Maybe this whole time I've been thinking that the wormhole needs to be this long mission, but it could be short, and it could work. Maybe—

There's a tap on my shoulder. "Quinn?"

I jump and open my eyes. There's no wormhole. My heart sinks. When I turn around, I see Ainsley and she's dressed in her team uniform. She's added bows to the top of her shin-guard socks.

"Cool costume," I say.

She shrugs. "I figured since I'm working the booth."

Her hair is in a waterfall braid. I bet Scarlett's mom did it. I touch my own tangled mess and wonder if I'm able to fix things when I come back, I'll also be wearing a team uniform and have a hairdo by Scarlett's mom.

We stare at each other awkwardly.

"Your banner looks nice."

"Oh, thanks."

"Sooo . . ." she says. "Have you checked out any of the booths? I'm thinking about joining recycling club in the spring. I think it might be fun."

I know I should say something nice like *Yeah, that does*

sound fun, or *That's an important cause*, but my brain feels like stones skipping over water.

"Have you seen Cora?"

Ainsley's face twists up into an even more awkward expression than before. "Wait. Are you guys still friends?"

The uncertainty of how to answer rattles in my chest. I play around with a couple of answers, but then I picture the giant oak tree—my giant oak tree, our giant oak tree, and I see that glowing door that I know is there if I can just make it appear—and I open my mouth and say, "Yes."

Then I take off to find her.

THIRTY-ONE
CORA

Here are some facts about thunder:

It is caused by the sudden increase in pressure and temperature that lightning produces.

Therefore, thunder does not exist without lightning.

In ancient times, people believed that thunder was the sound of gods stomping around. Or something like that.

In the nineteenth century, the accepted scientific theory was that lightning produced a vacuum. A vacuum is a space devoid of matter. A vacuum could theoretically be related to a wormhole.

That last fact is how I found a whole subthread of comments from people—people who I am going to assume are scientists—talking about how the likelihood of finding a wormhole is increased during a thunderstorm. This is because of the energy created by thunderstorms, and energy is what helps bring out "exotic matter." And "exotic matter" is what makes wormholes appear.

"Bingo," I say over and over again as I read through the thread. Mabel used to make fun of me for saying that. She said it made me sound like an old lady, which is fair. I probably picked it up from Grams.

Out of the corner of my eye, I see Mabel's empty bed. "Bingo," I repeat, looking at it for so long without blinking that my eyes begin to water.

I can't wait to say "bingo" to her again. I can't wait to tell her that it was a quote from our mom that helped me solve the mystery of how to bring her back. I absolutely can't wait.

I pull up the weather report for this week. Meteorology is, of course, not a precise science, but for this particular experiment I am going to have to rely on it.

I'm staring at the thunderstorm icon hovering over today's date, when there's a knock on my door.

"Cora?" Grams opens the door without asking. The knock was my warning. That's how it works with Grams.

I push my wheelie chair away from my computer to face her. "Huh?"

Grams's eyes narrow with concern as she takes me in. I admittedly do look pretty rough. It's late in the afternoon and I'm still wearing my pajamas. My eyes are red from staring at the computer screen for hours on end, and my pajamas are covered with crumbs from the granola bar I ate for lunch.

"Cora London," Grams says. "What project are you working on now?"

I wince as she turns on the light. I've been working in the dark. Something about the glow of the computer helps me concentrate.

"It's nothing."

Grams makes a disbelieving clicking sound with her tongue. "It doesn't look like nothing. It looks like it's running you ragged. Have you eaten anything of substance all day?"

Before I can answer, Dad walks into the room. He looks a little bit rough, too. His pants are wrinkled and he has ink splotches on his hands. It must be a grading weekend.

"You don't look ready for the fall festival," Dad says. It's then that I notice he's holding a camera. And not the type that comes with your phone, but the real deal.

"What?"

"Grams called me in here to see you off to the festival," Dad says.

"It's the fall festival tonight. A Chestnut Middle School tradition," Grams says.

"Um, I know what it is." I cross my arms over my chest. I look down at my crumb-covered pajamas. "But I'm clearly not going."

"Yes, Cora London. You are going." Grams stands up

from her chair. "I insist on it. I'm sure Junior Quiz Bowl is counting on you to help out at their booth."

Considering I've missed the last two practices, I don't think they're counting on anything from me. I sink lower into the wheelie chair. "I didn't volunteer to staff it. And I'm not ready. I don't even have a—"

She cuts me off and reaches behind her chair. "A costume? Lucky for you, I have that taken care of. I've spent the past few weeks making this for you."

She holds out a black headband with cat ears and a knitted black sweater with a matching knitted skirt. It's admittedly very cute and very much my style if I were going to go to the fall festival, which I most definitely am not.

I sigh. "That's really nice of you of you but—"

She cuts me off again. "Corrie, I don't ask you for a lot of things. But I'm asking you for this."

"Why?"

"Because it's an important moment. And I know this past year has been unbearably hard, and you've been robbed of so many things—" Grams's voice breaks a little, and I feel my insides softening. Sometimes I get the mashed potato feeling around Grams, too. "And I'll be damned if I let you be robbed of this moment."

The curse word makes me stand at attention. Grams never swears.

Dad clears his throat. "I'm in agreement with her."

I roll my eyes a little. "Of course you are."

Dad smiles faintly. "It would mean a lot to both of us if you went."

I grab the cat costume out of Grams's hands. "Fine."

Dad's smile turns to teasing. "And it would also be nice if you took a shower?"

I make a face back at him as I head up the stairs. "Noted."

And so that's how I find myself a few hours later being driven by Dad to the fall festival in the cat costume that Grams made me when it's one of the last places I want to be going. All I want is to be back at my computer, researching the connection between thunderstorms and time travel, obsessively refreshing the weather report. But because I haven't yet been able to time-travel and make everything okay again, I'm still the only Hamed girl.

And because I'm the only one, I can't make Grams and Dad sad. I can't disappointment them. I just won't.

Dad turns on the car's blinking lights and idles in front of the school. "I know we forced you into this," he says. "And as a general rule, I'm against doing that. But I think in this case, it was the right thing to do."

I frown. "Why?"

"Because you need to live your life, Cora." He looks back at me. "You can't keep waiting for your sister to come back."

That last sentence is like a punch in the gut.

But she's going to come back, my brain hisses. *I'm going to make her come back.*

He presses two fingers to his forehead. "Kiddo, do you understand what I'm saying?"

I run my hands along the car door. "I guess." Maybe I should just tell him about my time-travel plan. He might even be willing to help me. After all, he told me he thinks it's possible.

He reaches over me and opens the door. "So on that note, please go have fun, right?"

"Nothing says fun more than a forced event."

He gives me the world's saddest smile. "At the very least, the experience should help you grow. And I'm in the growing business."

I raise an eyebrow. "I thought you were in the advanced biology business."

"That too." His smile gets a little less sad. "Which I could argue in a way is also the growing business. But I meant parenting. It's my job to help you grow. Even when you don't want to."

"It's not that I don't want to grow . . ."

"I know," he says, and I can hear in his voice that he does.

I give him a small wave and get out of the car. I see lots of my classmates walking inside. They are all wearing elaborate costumes and I can practically see the excitement bouncing off them like energy waves.

I protectively cross my arms over my chest as I head to the door. I figure I'll stay for a couple of minutes and then duck out. What Grams and Dad don't know won't hurt them.

I follow the crowd to the gym, which has been transformed into an explosion of Halloween decorations. There's a witch's cauldron filled with dry ice, several elaborate paper pumpkin and acorn banners, and a large spiderweb over the bleachers. Despite my intentions of hating every second of this, I find myself smiling. I'm starting to remember why I used to love the fall festival.

"You came."

I turn around and see Spider-Man standing behind me.

"It's me," Owen says, pulling off his mask.

My smile widens. "I figured. Neat costume."

Owen's obsession with Spider-Man stems from a fascination with spiders. Most people care about the superhero stuff, but Owen's obsessed with the insect. He can go on and on about how underappreciated spiders are.

Sort of related: I've listened to him and Mia talk for hours about how insects are the key to solving global hunger. Basically Owen thinks all bugs are awesome. Me, though, I get why insects are important for our ecosystem, but spiders still make me queasy. And I'm definitely not that into the idea of eating crickets.

He balls up the mask in his hand. "Mia asked me if I thought you'd come."

"What'd you say?"

He looks at the gym floor. "I said I wasn't sure."

I bop my cat ears. They wiggle on my head. "Well, here I am."

I wait for him to ask me why I've missed the last couple of practices, but he doesn't. Instead he says, "Wanna check out the Quiz Bowl booth?"

"Sure," I say, and follow him through the swarms of people.

During PE, the gym always feels so cavernous. PE is the only class I absolutely detest, but now the gym feels less like a place of forced torture and way more like a party. For just a second, I forget all about time travel and wormholes and Mabel. But then I remember. And I feel bad for forgetting for even a moment.

"Cora!" Mia says, waving to me as we approach the booth. She's standing between Peter Tolbin and Molly Waldheim. All three of them are dressed like robots and they're standing in front of a neat stack of organized flyers. A diorama with information about Junior Quiz Bowl is propped up behind them. There's even a clear sparkling bowl filled to the brim with fun-sized candy.

Coach Pearlman gives me a salute. "There you are."

I try to come up with a believable excuse for why I've missed the last two practices, but I can't. Thankfully, Coach Pearlman doesn't press me.

But Mia does. She pulls me aside and Owen comes with us.

"Where have you been?" She puts her hands on the sides of her cardboard robot body.

"Since when are you close enough to Peter and Molly to wear matching costumes?"

"How about since you totally blew us all off and stopped even coming to practice?" she snaps back.

I look at Owen, but he doesn't meet my eye. He's pretending like the gym floor is the most interesting thing in the whole world.

"I only missed two practices." I let out a breath. "Besides, I've been busy with something."

Her eyes look like they could shoot lasers. And I don't think that's just because she's dressed up as a robot. "With Quinn?"

"No," I say sharply. "Not with Quinn."

"I thought you guys were hanging out."

I shake my head and curl my hands into fists. I can't talk about Quinn right now. "I've been researching something on my own."

"And what's that?"

My throat is dry. I swallow. "The shape of thunder."

Both Mia and Owen wrinkle their foreheads in thought. Owen massages his temples. "Isn't thunder shapeless?"

"Yes, technically. But try to think about it theoretically. What do you think it would look like?"

I take in their confused faces.

"Think about it," I press. "You're pushing your brain to stretch beyond what it thinks it knows. What I'm trying to say is, don't you think the shape of thunder might be similar to the shape of time?"

"And why would we want to know the shape of time?" Mia says.

I hesitate and bite the inside of my cheek. "I don't know. I think that maybe figuring out the shape of time is the key to time travel. And if the shape of thunder is similar to the shape of time, then it is all connected. Do you get what I'm saying?"

"You just made, like, a million leaps. My head is dizzy," Mia says.

"It does seem a little bit like a stretch," Owen agrees.

"But wait. Why are you so interested in time travel?" Mia asks.

For a brief moment, I lock eyes with Owen. And I get a feeling that he understands why, but he keeps his mouth shut. I look away from them both.

"This song," he says. He points at one of the large speakers in the gym. "It's pretty cool. Would you guys want to dance?"

I follow his eyes to the small group of kids dancing in the back corner of the gym. My stomach flips. For a second, I forget all about thunder and time travel and wormholes. I'm about to say yes when Mia gestures at her robot costume.

"Um, no. This box is not suitable for dancing."

I wait for him to ask me specifically, but he doesn't. The moment seems to be gone.

"All I was saying is it's interesting to think about the shape of thunder. And the shape of time," I say, but my voice sounds smaller than a microparticle.

"Well, I think time travel is a lot more complicated than just figuring out the 'theoretical' shape of thunder," Mia says, making actual air quotes with her fingers.

Right then, I hear a big boom of thunder. It rattles through the whole gym. At first, I think it might just be in the song. But a moment later, there's another boom. Even bigger this time. So big that everyone pauses talking and looks around.

"It's like it heard you talking about it," Owen says with a small grin.

I can't quite believe it. The weather forecast from this afternoon had predicted storms, but not until later. And the likelihood had only been 30 percent. Life has done me wrong in so many ways, but I can recognize a gift when I see one.

Another crash of thunder. "Hey," I say, already walking away. "I have to go."

THIRTY-TWO
QUINN

Dear Parker,

Sometimes I feel like Mom can't decide how she feels about me. One moment I'll catch her looking at me with so much love. And then another second, I'll see her watching me with fear.

I wish she could look at my face without being afraid.

Maybe if I can actually follow through with this plan, she'll be able to.

She'll be able to look at us both.

Can you imagine that?

Your sister,
Quinn

I weave my way through the crush of people, constantly murmuring apologies for bumping into someone's shoulder or knocking their costume's wig out of place.

"Ah. Sorry," I say for the hundredth time as I collide with a robot.

"Quinn."

I look up at the robot's face. It's Mia. Cora's friend. "Oh, Mia. Hi."

"Hi." Her voice is clipped and blunt. "Have you seen Cora? Do you know where she went?"

"Actually," I say, leaning back on my heels, "I was just looking for her."

"She left," another voice says.

I turn and see that Cora's other friend Owen is standing beside Mia. He's dressed like Spider-Man but is carrying the mask in a balled-up mess in his fist.

"Left? I didn't even think she was here."

"She said she had to go do something. And we thought she might be meeting you," Mia says. She's glowering at me.

Mia and I have never really gotten along. To be completely honest, I've always thought she was pretty snobby and didn't like me only because I'm not the type of kid who gets to go to the special pizza parties for straight-A students or gets invited to do the Talented and Gifted projects after school.

"Nope. Not me."

"But you guys have been hanging out a lot recently."

I decide not to update Mia that Cora and I aren't exactly on speaking terms right now. "I don't know where she is. Maybe she just went home? She doesn't really like crowds."

"I know that," Mia says. "But I thought she'd want to help with the Quiz Bowl booth."

I shrug. "I wouldn't know about that."

Mia gives me a look that spells out *obviously*.

"We're worried about her," Owen offers. Owen has always been nicer to me than Mia.

My eyes widen and a panic builds inside of me. "Worried? Why?"

A sharp thud of thunder makes everything in the gym shake. People fidget with that nervous energy that comes when they think there might be danger, but not actual life-threatening danger. It's something I used to do, too.

I don't find any bit of danger exciting anymore.

"She wouldn't stop talking about thunder," Mia says with a slight roll of her eyes. Mia doesn't seem that worried. I want to find that reassuring, but I don't.

"Well, with the shape of it," Owen explains. "Have you ever heard her talk about that before?"

"No." I rack my brain. "I mean, she had a pretty deep weather pattern obsession when we were in third grade."

"Oh, I remember that," Mia says.

I resist rolling my own eyes.

"She kept saying that figuring out the shape of thunder

237

was the key to figuring out the shape of time, which was the key to—"

"Time travel," I finish Owen's sentence.

Maybe she felt the same magic that I did here in this crowded and overdecorated gym. My pulse races. I turn on my heel. "I have to go," I say.

"Wait. Not you, too," Mia says.

"I know where she went. And I'm going to go find her."

"We're coming with you."

"No," I say. "This is between Cora and me."

"But—" Mia protests.

"It's between us," I repeat, more firmly this time.

"Well, let us know if you need something?" Owen offers, his eyes darting all around. "I mean, if you want—"

"Sure," I say. I don't wait for him to finish. I'm already running to find Cora.

THIRTY-THREE

CORA

The rain is coming down harder and harder. It seems like the faster I run, the more it rains. I finally make it into the woods. The tall trees lessen the impact a little, but I'm still getting drenched.

Plus, the rain impairs my vision. I can only see a few inches in front of my face.

I run faster and try not to think about the mud that's coating my sneakers and climbing up my ankles. I wipe the raindrops away from my eyes.

In the dark, it's hard to figure out where I am. All the trees have begun to look the same. It's like I'm running in circles. There's a loud boom of thunder. I jump.

I exhale. I shouldn't be scared. This is what I'm here for. The thunder and the energy it generates. The vacuum. The exotic matter.

I can't let myself get scared off.

When I was younger, I was really afraid of thunderstorms. Whenever we had a really bad storm, Mabel would let me crawl into her bed. She would hold me while the storm raged outside our window, gently rubbing my back. She'd always say, "Don't worry. It's just the sky putting on a show."

Of course, when I got older, I learned what actually causes a thunderstorm. But right now, as I'm standing in the pouring rain, I whisper to myself, "It's just the sky putting on a show."

I hear her words—her voice—in my head. It's like she's here with me, and so I keep running.

Her voice is clearer than it's been in months. Her rounded vowels and sharp consonants—she spoke with such a distinct rhythm. But recently, it's been harder for me to remember exactly how she sounded. I'll try to hear her but then I'll recall something that I know isn't her voice, but my own memory of it. It's the worst thing when your memories turn into memories themselves. Becoming unreliable duplicates of the real thing.

But right now, it truly sounds like Mabel. She's here with me.

"I'm coming!" I shout out into the rain. "I'm coming for you, Mabel."

I run farther and farther into the woods. The rain pounds down. The sky is inky black, crackling with the occasional strike of lightning. I only realize I've reached the creek when I hear it—the water is racing so loudly that it sounds alive.

"Cora!" a voice screams.

It's another voice I know. But it's not my sister.

"Cora!" the voice screams again.

I cup my hand over my eyes, looking all around. I can make out a shadowy figure running toward me.

"Cora, stop!"

It's Quinn.

"What are you doing here?"

"I'm here—I'm he-here for you."

Rain drips down my face. I don't have time for this. "I don't want you here."

"It's not safe to be out here in the storm." Quinn is closer now, but she's still shouting. "We need to go home."

"I don't need safety advice from you. Where was this concern when your brother was playing with your dad's guns?"

A crash of thunder shakes the forest. Quinn is quiet.

"That's what I thought," I say. I eye the creek. The water rushes with a loud roar.

"Core, I'm so sorry. I'm so, so sorry about everything. About Parker—"

"About Parker? You can't even say it! Your brother KILLED my sister. Quinn, do you not get it?" My eyes prick with tears. My throat is tight. I feel like I can't breathe.

Focus, I remind myself. I stare at the tree that's just

across the creek. I have to get there. I have to make things right.

"He did," Quinn says, her voice breaking a little. "I know he did, but—"

"There's no but," I say. "Don't you get it?"

"I do," Quinn says, and her voice sounds thick with tears, but I can't make out her face through the rain.

"Do you, though? I don't think you do. And until you do, you can't help me. I'm going to fix this all on my own—"

"Core, I don't know if we can—"

There's another crash of thunder. It rattles my bones. All I want right now is my sister. I want her to rub my back. I want her to tell me that the sky is only putting on a show.

"Don't you dare say it," I say. "Don't you dare tell me that I can't fix it. I have to be able to fix it. I have to."

My throat is raw from screaming and my eyes are blurry from the rain. "I have to do this. If—" I won't even say it. I won't voice any doubt. I stretch my foot out to the first rock.

My sneaker slips, but I make it.

"Cora!" Quinn yells. "Don't!"

"I'm going to do this, Quinn. You'll see."

The creek water rushes up around my ankles. It's freezing cold.

I squint to try and make out the shadowy outline of the next rock I'll need to jump to in order to make it across.

I can do this.

I have to do this. I have to do this for Mabel.

I jump. I hear Quinn scream.

There is a rush of water. I see my sister's face.

I see her. I see her. I see her.

THIRTY-FOUR
QUINN

Dear Parker,

I can't fix what you did.

I'll never understand it.

It will never be okay.

Your sister,
Quinn

It's like something out of a horror film. It happens so fast, but it's also painfully slow—Cora jumping to the next rock, slipping, and hitting her head with a sickening thud. The sound of her skull colliding with the rocks is something I will never ever be able to forget. No matter how much I want to.

My body reacts before my mind. I run toward the creek. The water is up to my waist as I reach out for her. The current pushes against me, threatening to shove me downstream.

"Cora! Cora! Cora!" I shout, but she doesn't answer me.

The water is rushing over her body. Her head lolls, dipping into the current.

I grab her wrist, tightly wrapping my fingers around it. She doesn't move. I keep pulling, trying to drag her to me, but she is so heavy.

"Cora," I say, her name catching in my throat. "Cora, I can't lose you. Cora, come on." I reach out to gently slap her cheek. She doesn't move. "You're my best friend, Cora. You're my favorite person. I've never told you this, you— you—you—"

I don't know how to quite say what I want to say. I picture us sitting together in the back of Grams's station wagon on the way to preschool, Cora holding my hand because she knew I was nervous. Riding our bikes together down the street, me jumping off mine to help her stay steady, to keep her from falling. Sleepover after sleepover, our backs spine-to-spine as we talked and talked. Cora and me, Coraandme, always Cora.

She still doesn't move. I scream and pull at her, grabbing everywhere and anywhere. My head goes underwater for a moment. I surface and gasp for air.

I tread to keep my place. The water roars all around us.

It shoves at my sides, pushing and pushing at me, my feet slip, but I catch myself. I scream again—bellowing at the creek, at the thundering sky, at my brother, at the world.

I bend at my knees and channel every bit of strength I have, lunging toward Cora in an attempt to hoist her out of the creek.

It fails.

She's lying facedown in the creek. I roll her over quickly. The current surges around us. Her body is so limp and water is dribbling out of her mouth. Water slaps against my face. I scream over and over again. My heart pounds so fast that I think it might jump out of my chest.

"Cora!" I scream again, grabbing both of her arms and dragging them through the water. We are smacked and bruised by the current, but this time, I make it to shore.

I fall down beside her, hardly able to catch my breath, my lungs hiccuping as they try to catch up with my heart. Pressing my head against Cora's chest, I check for a pulse. Every part of my body tenses in anticipation. "Cora?" I whisper.

She doesn't answer, but her inhales and exhales do. My eyes swell up with tears. I let out a loud sob.

"It's going to be okay," I tell her. "It's going to be okay."

I don't know how it is, but I'm going to find a way.

We're going to find a way. Cora and me. Coraandme.

THIRTY-FIVE
CORA

When I open my eyes, the first thing I see is a blinking light. I don't know where I am, and in my confusion, I whisper, "Mabel?"

A hand grabs mine. It is bigger than I remember my sister's. The grip is firmer. But a warm feeling of hope runs through me. "Mabel," I say again.

"*Alhamdulillah,*" the voice says. As my vision sharpens, I see my dad's face. There is stubble on his cheeks and dark circles under his eyes. He keeps squeezing my hand and bows his head over my body. "Cora. My Cora. You're awake."

I sit up a little, but he cautions me to stay still. "You've been through so much. You need to rest."

"I need to find Mabel," I say. I look around at the white walls. I don't know where I've traveled back to. I'm not quite sure how I managed it either. I don't remember making it to the giant oak tree. I try to think back to the woods and the rain—

Dad interrupts my thoughts.

"Sweetie," he says softly. "Mabel . . . Mabel, she's not—" His voice cracks.

When I look at his face, the reality of the situation lands on me like a brick. I'm flattened by it.

I haven't time-traveled.

I'm in the exact same world I was before.

A world without my sister.

"What happened? Where am I?" Those questions burn like acid in my throat. I don't want to have to ask. Asking means that I've failed.

"Quinn found you in the woods. You fell in the creek. She called the paramedics." Dad squeezes my hand again. I wince at how hard his grip is. "Thank goodness Quinn was there. She saved your life."

I blink. "What?"

Dad tilts his head to look at me. "What were you doing in the woods?"

I contemplate lying. But as I stare at the plain white walls, I can't bring myself to do it. "I was trying to time-travel. I was trying to save Mabel."

Dad doesn't say anything. I can feel his pulse change in his hand. It quickens.

"That probably sounds silly, but you told me it was

possible. You said I just needed to figure out the shape of thunder, which would lead me to the shape of time."

"Oh, Cora," he says, and his face looks so impossibly sad.

I feel impossibly stupid.

"But I couldn't pull it off. I don't know why. I just . . ." My voice is shaky. My voice is never shaky, but I don't know how to manage these words. "I just wanted to fix things so badly."

Dad leans over and gently strokes the top of my head. "Kiddo, it's not your job to fix anything."

I shake my head. My throat tightens to the point I'm not sure I can breathe. Let alone talk.

"It's okay. Calm down," Dad says.

"I don't want to calm down!" I jerk away from him. A wire that's attached to me snags, I feel a sting in my wrist.

"Calm down," he repeats.

I stay still, but I frown at him. "I'm so tired of people saying it's not my job to fix things. No one else is fixing them."

Dad hangs his head. "I know. You're right. And I'm so sorry."

"For what? You didn't do anything. I'm the one who ran into the woods in the middle of a storm because I thought the energy from the thunder would help me." I shake my head as though I can get rid of my embarrassment, but it doesn't work. "I was trying to figure out the shape of thunder. I thought if I found that, I'd find the shape of time. And then I'd be able to . . ." I trail off and look at the white hospital wall. "I'm sorry."

"That's right. I didn't do anything." He reaches for my hand again. "And I'm the one who should be sorry. I should've been better. I should've talked with you more honestly so that you would've understood this wasn't something that you could fix. Your sister is gone, Cora. It is a tragedy. An unspeakable tragedy. But she is gone, and I'm so, so sorry."

His words are like the slamming of a door. The final grade on an exam.

Mabel's death feels more real to me in this moment than it ever has. Even when I watched her get lowered into the ground, there was a part of me that didn't believe that was my sister in that white cloth shroud.

But now—now I've run out of places to hide. This room suddenly feels very small like the walls are closing in on me. I let out a strangled sound.

Dad's eyes fill with concern. He keeps holding on to my hand. "I know it's hard, Cora. And I should've . . . I should've talked with you more. I should've never let it get to this point."

"It just doesn't seem right that there's nothing we can do."

Dad fidgets. His feet shuffle on the ground. "That's one

of the hardest things about death. It's never going to be okay, but we'll always have our love for her. And we'll always have the love she had for us."

"She's really gone."

Dad wipes his eyes. "She's really gone. But she's also still with us. Her love, our love, we have that. It's with us."

I look at the wires that are attached to my body. I watch the beeping on the monitor. The jagged lines that show I'm alive. The line that's now flat for my sister. That will always be flat. "Can I tell you something?"

"Of course, kiddo. Anything."

I roll my tongue over my teeth. "You and Grams always say those things. Like we'll always have our love. And I know that. I do. But it still doesn't make it seem okay. I guess what I'm trying to say is that I understand those things and those phrases, but I also don't."

Dad pinches the space between his eyebrows. He lets out a deep breath. "I get what you're saying. And I'm not sure what to say. But I'm going to offer this up, and if it's not helpful, feel free to ignore me."

I give him a tiny, teasing smile. "Mabel was always better at that."

"True," Dad says with a laugh that's more sad than happy. "So, in the world of science, we have imperfect theories that are still studied and accepted. Have I ever talked to you about this before?"

I shake my head.

"Well, it's discussed a lot when we talk about Newton's laws of motion and universal gravitation. The theory that Newton came up with works. By that, I mean it bears out mathematically. You can chart it. But as we started to learn more about the world, we realized that what Newton philosophized isn't at all what's actually happening with the particles on a physical level. And Newton's laws of motion were replaced with Einstein's theory of relativity, and someday, Einstein's theory of relativity may be replaced. Scientific knowledge, as a whole, is basically a collection of imperfect theories that are always changing and evolving as we learn more about the universe."

"Okay . . ." I say slowly, not quite sure I'm understanding, even though I really want to.

"So maybe you can think of how you're handling missing Mabel—how you're coping with your grief—as an imperfect and evolving theory. It's always something you're going to have to puzzle over. But the ideas, the theories, of the comforting things that Grams says can be helpful. Because they work, even if they don't actually, well, you know, work. Like Newton's laws of motion. They are imperfect and incomplete, but that doesn't stop them from being useful or worthwhile. There's a reason you still study Newton in school." Dad scratches his head.

He continues. "What I'm trying to say is that your

feelings, and your feelings about your feelings, can evolve with you. And it's okay for them to do that. It actually could be said that it is scientific for them to do that."

"Feelings about feelings," I repeat, and give him a smile. "That explanation is the most annoying science-professor thing ever, and I actually like it."

"I thought you might."

"Mabel would not like it at all."

"Probably not," Dad says, and I see that his eyes are full of tears again. He touches my chin. "I love you so much. You know that, right?"

I nod. He lets go of my chin.

"And you're growing up. Growing up is like an imperfect theory in its own way."

My throat is dry. I understand what Dad's saying, but there's only one thought in my brain. I decide to say it.

"Mabel's never going to get to grow up."

Dad's eyes overflow again. Tears run down his cheeks. "No. She's not."

"That makes me so sad."

"Me too."

"But it makes me happy to talk about her."

Dad nods.

"We should talk about her more," I say.

Dad nods again. "Okay."

"Do you promise?"

"I promise."

"Hey, Dad?"

"Yeah?"

"I know there's nothing we can do to bring back Mabel." I stare down at my bruised hands and remember the stormy sky from last night. "But there has to be something we can do."

"What do you mean?"

"To try and make sure what happened to Mabel doesn't happen again."

Dad is silent for a while. He doesn't look at me.

"Dad?"

"That one is so tricky, Cora. More than anything, I want to make sure what happened to Mabel doesn't happen again."

"Then why don't we do something? Why don't we do something to change things?"

He runs his hand through his hair. "It's complicated, Corrie."

Complicated. Moaqqad. I hate that word. The fact that I know how to say it in Arabic only marginally makes me dislike it less. "That's what grown-ups say when they don't want to tell the truth."

Dad squints in thought.

"Hey, Dad?"

"Yeah?"

"Can I ask you one last question?"

"You can always ask me as many questions as you have."

I give him a nervous smile. "Do you believe in impossible things? I mean, even with everything that's happened. Do you still believe in impossibly good things?"

"Of course," Dad says without hesitation. He kisses me on the top of the head. "And I believe in you, Cora. I believe in you."

THIRTY-SIX
QUINN

Dear Parker,

It didn't work.

I don't know why I'm still writing you. You're never going to read these letters, are you?

You're never going to know how furious I am at you.

You're never going to know how much I hate you.

You're never going to know how much I loved you.

You're never going to know.

Your sister,
Quinn

I haven't come out of my room since I got home. Cupcake's stayed by my side almost the whole time. That's one nice thing about cats—they understand the idea that you can want to be alone, but not actually alone.

This is something Mom doesn't get. She knocks on my door every once in a while, coming in with trays of food that I don't touch. I listen when she tells me that Cora's dad called from the hospital with the news that Cora is going to be okay, but I don't say anything.

Cora isn't going to be okay. How do they not get that?

It's not okay. It's not okay at all.

I was supposed to make it okay, and I didn't.

So when Mom comes into my room again, I'm prepared for a tray filled with mini cheese quiches and some meaningless optimistic comment that I know she doesn't even believe, but instead she hovers in the doorway, staring hard at me, not saying a thing.

I keep scratching the space between Cupcake's ears, listening to her purr, and thinking about how I wish I could make a sound like that. A sound that said, *Don't leave, don't leave, please don't leave.*

"Why were you in the woods?" Mom asks. Her voice is shy.

Cupcake's fur is soft between my fingers. I don't answer Mom, and before I know it, Dad's also in my room. They're both standing near the door like we're playing that game we used to play when I was little—hot lava—where we avoid the molten center of the carpet. I wish I was little again. When the imaginary lava was on the carpet and not inside of me.

"Did you ask her?" Dad says to Mom like I'm invisible.

"She's not saying anything," Mom whispers in a way that lets me know that she knows that I can hear.

I still don't say a word.

"Q," Dad says. His voice has none of Mom's uncertainty. "What were you doing with Cora in the woods?"

I shrug. "She's my friend." I refuse to use the word *was* instead of *is*, even though was is probably more accurate. My eyes drop to my paisley bedspread that Mom picked out when I was ten. It's pretty and I've always liked it, but it's starting to feel all wrong. Like I'm no longer the type of person who should have a paisley bedspread. I don't know who that type of person is exactly, but I'm pretty sure she isn't the sister of Parker McCauley.

"I thought—" Dad clears his throat. "I thought I told you to be careful about hanging out with her. Because of what happened."

I lift my chin. "And what did happen?"

Dad's skin flushes red, and he clears his throat again. "Don't be smart with me, young lady. Your mother and I are trying to talk to you. You know we can't afford for you to get into any trouble. Especially not—"

"Because of what happened." My eyes meet his. I can see the surprise. I'm not the type of kid who has ever finished sentences.

"I'm warning you, Quinn," Dad says.

Mom grips his arm. "Daniel," she hisses.

"What?" he says. "She's being ridiculous."

I sit up farther, which makes Cupcake jumps off the bed. I wish she wouldn't leave.

"I—I—I—" I wince. This isn't the time for a Freeze-Up.

Dad waves his hand in the air. It's a simple gesture, a slight brushing, but it sets off something inside of me. The hot lava.

"You're the one who killed things for fun. You had the guns for that, right? For fun! And I'm the one who is being ridiculous? How come—" My teeth are almost chattering from the burning that's swimming around inside me. "How come we never talk about that? How come we never talk about anything? We just pretend. And maybe that's what I was doing in the woods. Pretending."

Saying those words aloud makes me feel so alone. I really wish Cupcake was still next to me. I wish anyone was next to me. I hug my stomach and breathe through the tears that I can't stop anymore. My face burning with shame as I cry.

"Oh, honey," Mom says. She takes a tiny step toward me, but she still feels miles away.

"I saw Parker with the guns," I say. "I saw him. I knew."

"Oh, honey," Mom repeats. "No. No, you didn't."

"I did." I put my hands over my face. The tears won't stop. "It's my fault."

Mom sits down next to me. She doesn't hug me, but it feels good to know she's closer. "It's not your fault, Quinn."

"But I knew." When I look up, I see that Dad is still standing in the doorway. His eyes are glossy and unfocused, and he's fiddling with his watch.

Mom shakes her head firmly. "It's not your fault. I didn't know you felt that way. Why didn't you tell us this before?"

I press the heel of my hand against my eyes. "How would you? You never let me talk."

She leans away from me. "That's not true, honey. I've always been so patient with you. You can't say that."

"I just did."

"Okay, well—"

"Mom, we never talk about what actually happened. We never talk about why it happened. We pretend like it didn't. No one in this family ever takes any responsibility. And it's—" I pull at clumps of my hair. "It's hurting me."

"Oh, oh, oh," Mom says. She puts her hand over her mouth. "I don't know what to say."

I stare at my corkboard filled with my soccer things, the hamburger menu, and all my photos of me and Cora. "I don't know either."

"What do you want me to do?"

I look her right in the eye. "I want to talk with some-one about this. Someone professional." I say the word Mrs. Euclid used. *Professional*. It sounded like someone who could really help. I don't know if Mrs. Euclid called Mom. I hope she didn't. But I also kind of hope she did.

"No," Dad says. "I don't think that's a good idea."

"Daniel," Mom says. "Let's listen to Quinn."

"Fine," Dad says. He doesn't look at me. "I'll think about it, okay?"

He casts one last look at Mom and then walks out of the room.

"This is hard for your dad, Quinn," Mom says.

"It's hard for me, too. Don't you get that? I've tried— I've—I've—"

She wraps her arm around my shoulder. Gently, she wipes the tears from my cheek and meets my gaze.

"Okay, Quinn, okay. We'll go talk to someone."

"Really?"

"Really." She puts her hand on top of mine and it feels like a promise.

It feels like a start.

THIRTY-SEVEN
CORA

Mia comes to visit on the second day I'm home from the hospital. She brings me all the homework and assignments that I've missed. I'm supposed to go back next week, but Dad says I can take as long as I want. Really, I'm ready to get back to school. Sitting alone all day in my room—in my and Mabel's room—isn't making me feel any better.

"If you want, I can talk you through it," Mia says once she's done going over everything I've missed in math.

"That's okay. I'm sure I can figure it out."

Mia digs around some more in her backpack. "Well, I think I've given you everything."

I cross my legs, feeling a little embarrassed that it's the late afternoon and I'm still in my pajamas. "Thanks again for coming over."

She tugs on the ends of her hair. It's already grown a lot

since she chopped it all off a few months ago. "Of course. I was, you know, worried about you. I'm really glad you're okay. I mean, you are okay, right?" She gives me her searching look.

I shrug. "I'm here."

"You know what I mean," Mia says.

I look down at the pile of papers she brought me. "Yeah. I know."

"It's just, well, I don't want to make you mad or anything."

"Mia, it's okay. I'm not like a breakable object now."

"Right, right. I know we were fighting before. And I just wanted to say that I'm sorry. I get . . . well, you know how I get. We've been friends a long time, right?" she says, letting out a nervous-sounding laugh.

"Right," I answer.

"I don't know. I've always been kind of jealous of you and Quinn. Like you always had this thing that you and I didn't have." Her eyes dart around the room. My skin begins to crawl when I realize she's looking at Mabel's bed.

There's a drumming sound in my ears and I'm pretty sure it's my pulse. "Mia, I don't know what you want me to say."

"It's just I knew you had all these things going on with what happened to your sister, and Owen—"

"Mia, come on," I say, throwing my head back.

"No, you come on. I know you, Cora. I'm not completely clueless."

At that, I cross my arms. Now I'm folded up like a pretzel. "I never said you were."

"I don't know, but to me, it felt like you were talking to Quinn about all these things and I just wanted you to know you could talk to me. That's all."

I hang my head and stare at my crossed legs. It makes me think of preschool and how our teacher would say, "Sit crisscross, applesauce." Which for some reason made Quinn laugh, which would make me laugh because back then I always laughed when she laughed.

I blow out a breath. "Mia, you're my really good friend. And Quinn is, too. But to be honest, I haven't been talking to anyone about those things. Especially not Owen."

"By the way, Owen was really sorry he couldn't come today. He had to babysit Erika," Mia says.

I try to hide my smile, but it comes anyway. "Yeah, he texted me."

"And?" Mia prompts.

"He texted me some funny animal videos to watch if I got bored."

"And?"

I wrinkle my nose. "The one with the flying squirrels was hilarious. Want me to send it to you?"

Mia laughs. "I'm not talking about videos."

I throw my hands around in the air helplessly. "You know."

"I think I do, but I want to confirm my theory."

"Your theory?"

"You know what I mean," Mia says. "How you feel about Owen."

I squirm, crossing and uncrossing my ankles. "I just don't know."

"But you think he's cute, right?"

I cover my hands with my face. "Yeah. I think so. I guess."

Mia laughs a little, and I fall back onto my pillow and shield my face. "This is so embarrassing."

"Yeah, well, I'm about to tell you something embarrassing, too."

"What?"

"I think Peter Tolbin is cute."

"What?" I scrunch up my face. "Peter Tolbin? But he wears so much of that body spray that smells like leather."

"I know, right?" Mia says, laughing nervously. "But seriously, hey, don't judge me. I mean, I think it smells kind of good."

I hold up my hands. "I'm not, I'm not, I'm not."

She flops down on the bed next to me. "It's totally weird, right? The feeling?"

"The weirdest."

"What do you think we should do about it?"

I stare at the ceiling and wonder about Mabel for the two hundredth time in the past hour. *You would know what to do*, I think.

"I don't know," I say quietly.

"Me either," Mia says.

"But you know what? I'm trying to get better at not knowing. Like for now, I'm happy just being friends with Owen."

Mia playfully jabs me in the side with her elbow. "Did I just hear you, Cora, say you're okay with not knowing something?"

I laugh. "That's even weirder, right?"

"Yeah, but I kind of like it."

Mia and I talk for a while more. She tells me all the reasons she thinks Peter Tolbin is cute. She, of course, has made a whole list of his attractive attributes.

We also talk about Quiz Bowl. We're probably not going to make the regional playoffs, which is a big bummer. But we still have a couple of meets left. I'm hoping that I'll be back at school in time to get to compete. Eventually Mia leaves, and I'm left alone again with a big pile of homework.

"What did she do, print off *Webster's Dictionary* or something?" Grams says when she walks into my room and sees the big stack of papers.

"No, Grams," I say. "Mia brought over all the

assignments I missed this week. And if she was going to print out a dictionary, Mia is more of an Oxford type of girl."

Grams shakes her head at me. "I'm not even going to laugh at that. I don't want to egg you on."

I laugh a little and look back at the pile. "It is pretty overwhelming."

"No rush, Cora London."

I don't bother trying to argue with Grams about how there is most definitely a rush because missing assignments can really tank your grade. Instead, I shrug. Grams sits down on Mabel's bed. My posture stiffens. I don't like when anyone touches Mabel's things and Grams knows that.

"So, honeybee, I'm going to say something and you aren't going to like it."

I groan a little. My guess is she's going to tell me my hair looks like the home of several blue jays and I am in desperate need of a shower. Both things are true, but I'd rather she not say them.

"No, no. Don't groan. What I'm about to say, it's serious."

I look up at her. "What?"

"I brought up some boxes. They're in the hallway."

A lump forms at the base of my throat. "Boxes?"

She pats Mabel's comforter. "To pack up. It's time, honey."

"But—" The lump quickly builds into a salty bile. I feel the familiar prick of tears.

"It's never going to be time, but also, it's time. You, holding on to it—well, that's only going to continue to tear you into two. And I won't let that happen. I need you whole. Your daddy needs you whole. The whole world needs you whole, my sweet Cora."

She stands up and walks toward me. She kisses me on the cheek. "You take your time. And if you want help, I'll gladly help. But I had a feeling you'd want to do it on your own."

I nod, but don't say anything because I don't trust my voice.

"You know, baby girl, we lose people. But we're found in people, too."

I frown at her.

"I'm saying that you lost your sister, and nothing in this whole wide world is ever going to make that okay, but I want you to also think a little about the love that saved you. The love that was there for you on that night when you needed it most. You have all that love, sweet pea. All of it. Mabel's love, your love for Mabel, but also that other love. And that's nothing to sneeze at."

She's talking about Quinn. I curl my hands into fists.

"It's been a long hard road, Corrie. And it's going to keep being hard. But I also know that you're going to keep being. That's a gift, baby. That's a gift, to keep being. I hope you see that. I hope you take that gift and run with it." She kisses the palm of her hand and then places it on my forehead.

I sit on my bed for a while after Grams leaves. I think about Newton's laws of motion. I think about Einstein's theory of relativity. I think about how two things can both be right. And I think about all the things that are wrong.

I think about how theories are really only theories. How they're imperfect guesses. How we never actually know anything for sure. One minute that makes me feel better. The next minute that makes me feel like garbage.

Time feels sticky and slow. I step out into the hallway. The sight of the boxes makes my heart sink deeper into my stomach. But I reach down and pick one up. I carry it into my room.

I grab a couple of Mabel's shirts out of her dresser. I run my fingers over the seams. I wonder about the last time she wore each shirt. What she was thinking when she wore it. I hate that I can't even remember her wearing some of the shirts. I tap my temples, but it doesn't jog my memory.

When my eyes land on the tubes of lip gloss, I feel my throat tighten all over again. I start to pack them up, but at the last moment, I slide one tube into my pocket. It's the one I brought with me to the giant oak tree. The shade she wore on the last morning she was alive.

I walk over to the small mirror that's on her side of the room. Slowly, I put on the lip gloss.

"I miss you so much," I whisper to the empty room.

I look at my reflection again. Seeing that plum color on my lips makes me feel like a part of my sister is still with me. I'm not packing up this lip gloss.

I carry the rest of the boxes into my room. There is so much stuff. Waddle, Mabel's stuffed penguin, stares at me from her bed.

I feel overwhelmed and very alone. I close my eyes. I hear Grams's words in my head and reach for the phone.

I call someone who I know will get it.

"Hello?" Quinn says, picking up after one ring.

"Can you come over? I need help."

She doesn't hesitate for even a second before saying, "I'm on my way."

THIRTY-EIGHT
QUINN

Dear Parker,

This is the last letter I'm ever going to write you.

I don't think I'll ever have the words to say exactly what I want to say. I don't think those words exist.

But I'm going to try.

I also know you're never going to read this letter. But I like to imagine that there's a world where you do. I'm sure Cora would tell me that's scientifically impossible, but I don't care. I want to believe it.

Cora told me that Grams says the dead belong to the living. She says that she means that it's the people who are alive who create the memory of the dead person. So it's my job to remember you.

The good and the bad. About your tipped-back head laugh. About how angry you would get. About how much you liked pickles. About all the hateful stuff you posted on the internet. About how you helped me down from the tree and those tears in your eyes. About how you once looked at me like you wanted to hurt me, like you wanted to hurt yourself. About how sometimes, when we were both little, you looked at me like I was your favorite person in the world.

I'm going to tell the truth because I hope that it saves another girl somewhere from having to write letters to her dead brother. I hope it means that she's able to help him in a way that I wasn't able to help you.

I think it's possible for me to love you and never excuse or forgive what you did. I didn't think that was possible before, but I'm choosing to believe that it is now.

Your sister,
Quinn

It was Cora's idea to visit the giant oak tree today. I didn't think it was such a great idea. I mean, I didn't want Cora to slip again. And also, I didn't feel ready to face everything, but Cora said that the date on the calendar—November 11—was going to make us face it anyway, so we might as well do it on our own terms.

That's a phrase she uses a lot. *Our own terms.* I'm still

not really sure what it exactly means, but I'm learning. Cora's been talking to me a lot about how learning is the most important thing we can do. That it is okay if we don't always know the perfect answer or the solution. At least that's what I think she's saying. I try to keep up with everything she tells me, but sometimes my mind still drifts.

We walk together to the giant oak tree. Cora talks about random things, and I nod here and there to let her know that I'm listening. I know that it helps her to talk, and she knows that it helps me to listen. She told me the other day that *silent* is an anagram for *listen*. An anagram is like a word scramble. It's when the letters used to write one word can be rearranged to write another. Cora likes anagrams. And I like that she is telling me about them, that she's telling me about things again.

The sky today is pale blue dotted with the fluffy harmless-looking type of cloud. A weak, watery type of sunlight leaks into the forest. Without their leaves, a lot of the trees look skeletal. The air is crisp and refreshing and smells faintly of smoke. When we reach the creek, I dart out in front of Cora.

"It's fine, Quinn. It's not storming. I've crossed it so many times by myself." She points at the water. "Look, it's so low. It hasn't rained in days."

"I know, but—" I hop out onto the first rock. I turn around and hold out my hand. I stare at the faint bruise by her temple. It's faded, but it's still there. "It'll make me feel better. Can we please do it, together?"

"Okay," she says, taking my hand.

We cross, hand in hand, step by step, and both stare at the tree. At its long branches, at its thick trunk. Even after everything that has happened, I still don't think I was wrong about it being magical.

Standing here, on this day, with Cora feels like proof of that.

I reach into my pocket where I've stashed my letters to Parker. Pulling them out, I crouch down near the base of the tree. I run my hands over the bump of its root, and search for a place where the soil is soft enough to dig. The cool air makes my fingers stiff, but I keep digging.

Beside me, Cora has already started to create a tiny hole. She scatters a packet of violet seeds into the soil while I bury my letters. Grams apparently warned her that the seeds aren't likely to take, but Cora told her she had a good feeling they would grow. Cora says she wants to see Mabel's favorite flower growing in an unlikely place. That's the closest I've gotten to hearing her say that she also still thinks the giant oak tree is magic.

We keep digging our holes side by side. One of us is letting something go; the other one is asking something to grow. Right now, I'm not sure there's that big of a difference between those two things.

Cora's pushing dirt on top of the seeds when she says, "Do you think you'll play soccer next year?"

I look up at the pale blue sky. There's a small flock of birds fluttering overhead. "I don't know."

"I do," Cora says with a small smile.

The birds chirp. *Life.* I glance at the giant oak tree. Sunlight glints off The Eyeball. And then I see it. Not the wormhole, but another kind of magic. Cora and me. Me and Cora. Coraandme.

I smile back at her. "Eureka."

AUTHOR'S NOTE

Stories have always been how I make sense of the world. Within the realm of stories—as both a reader and a writer—I am able to examine and grapple with the parts of life that I find the most difficult. Stories can be conversation starters. They can help break the ice about things that feel too scary or too hard to talk about.

This book started with my own fear of gun violence. The fear of it is something that keeps me up late at night—worrying about my own kids, worrying about my readers.

Gun violence affects so many young people, regardless of their zip code or skin color. It is true that when tragedies occur in communities like Quinn and Cora's, they often receive more attention than when tragedies happen in other less privileged communities, and that is not right. I want us to work together to make the world a safer place for all young people, no matter where they live.

I am frustrated with my and other grown-ups' willingness to simply accept gun violence as a normal part of life. Our inability to come up with solutions that are bolder and more comprehensive than lockdown drills, which are often anxiety producing. We know the problem is multipronged, and instead of rising to the challenge, we have buckled because of its seeming impossible complexity.

This is a book about imagining the impossible. About the power in that imagining. About bumping up against the edge of what we believe could be possible and envisioning more. Envisioning better. Toward the end of the book, Cora asks her dad if he still believes in impossibly good things. He responds that he believes in Cora. And I believe in *you*. I hope you'll join me in working toward a better and safer world. Progress can be frustratingly slow, but it can only happen if first we believe that it can.

If this book started with fear, it ended with love. Love for you, my reader. I want the world to be a better, safer place for you. As humans, love is our truest form of magic. I really believe that. Love, hope, and imagination can shape and change our world.

Change also begins with talking to one another, even if those conversations are difficult. It begins with sharing our fears, our frustrations, our love, and our ideas. I hope this book helps to open the conversation. I'm ready to listen to you.

Love,

Jasmine

To learn more about how to continue the conversation about gun violence, please visit:

www.momsdemandaction.org

www.everytown.org

www.bradyunited.org

www.sandyhookpromise.org

ACKNOWLEDGMENTS

Heaps and heaps of gratitude to:

Brenda Bowen, thank you for your steadfast belief in my stories, and for encouraging me to take risks and be bold. Love to the whole wonderful team at the Book Group. Thanks also to Stefanie Diaz and everyone at Sanford J. Greenburger Associates.

Alessandra Balzer, thank you for your sharp insights, your patience, and your warmth. My books are so much better for it. I'm beyond lucky to work with you. Lots of love to everyone at Balzer + Bray, especially Caitlin Johnson. It's truly such an immense honor to be published by you all.

The whole brilliant team at Harper Children's, especially Suzanne Murphy, Andrea Pappenheimer, Kathy Faber, Kerry Moynagh, Nellie Kurtzman, Vaishali Nayak, Patty Rosati, Jacquelynn Burke, Sam Benson, Ann Dye,

Katie Dutton, Stephanie Macy, Mimi Rankin, Laura Harshberger, Alice Wang, and Jenna Stempel-Lobell. Thank you for everything you do for my books. It never ceases to amaze me that a book only has one name on the cover, but it really should have several. I'm enormously grateful to all of you.

Thank you to all of my very thoughtful sensitivity readers. You made this book infinitely better, and I am forever grateful to you for your knowledge. I am always learning.

Thank you to everyone who agreed to read this manuscript early and whose early love of the book made me feel extra inspired to share Cora and Quinn's story with the world: John Schu, Rebecca Stead, Kathy M. Burnette, Cody Roecker, Jennifer Kraar, Melissa Posten, Jillian Heise, and Kathleen March.

This is the place where I would like to thank every bookseller, librarian, and educator who has supported and uplifted my work. There are too many of you to name, but please know just how grateful I am. Thank you for everything you do to get books into the hands of kids who need them.

Special shout-out to all the Windy City Readers. How lucky am I to be a part of such a wonderful group of book lovers?

Thank you to Phil Binder and the whole marvelous team at the Author Village.

I'm very fortunate to have the support of many friends.

Thanks in particular to Alexandra Perrotti, Emery Lord, Becky Albertalli, David Arnold, Adam Silvera, Kim Liggett, Rachel Strolle, Renee Sabo, Rachel Meyers, Nicole Hall, Lane West, Tyler West, Elysse Wagner, Kristan Hoffman, Erica Kaufman, Kelly Lawler, Dan Lawler, Connie Smith, Kt DeLong, Ashley Keyser, and Christopher Adamson.

Much love to my family on both sides of the Atlantic— the Nazeks, the Wagners, and the Wargas. In particular, thanks to my mother, Patricia Anne Nazek, my father, Mohammad Nour Nazek, and my brother, Brandon Khader Nazek.

Gregory Scott Warga, I never quite know how to say thank you. I don't ever have words that are expansive and full enough. So instead, I'll say: I love you. Infinitely.

Lillian Nour and Juniper Lee, I'm so lucky to be your mama. Thank you for all your wise and wonderful questions. And thank you for your patience while I drafted this book during a very hard year. Love you to the moon and back.

And to all my young readers, it is such an enormous privilege to write for you. I love you. I see you. I know you're going to change the world for the better. Eureka!

Turn the page for a sneak peek at Jasmine Warga's
new novel, *A Rover's Story*.

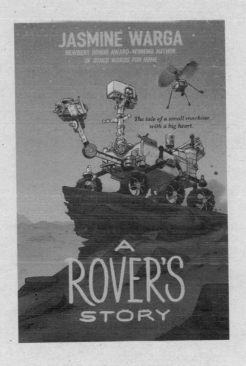

THE FIRST DAY

I am not born in the way humans are, but there is beginning. Beeping. Bright lights. A white room filled with figures in white hazmat suits. So much information to process, but I can handle it. I awake to knowledge. My circuits fire. The room cheers. A loud sound, but it does not startle me.

I am not built for startling. I have been built for observation.

In the sea of unknown figures, I focus on a face.

I do not know if I have a face. If I have one, my information suggests it is not like this one. This face has what humans call lips. The human lips curl upward.

A smile.

I cannot smile—this I know—but somehow I understand the significance of this expression. I am learning.

My mission has begun.

LEARNING

I am built to collect and process information. That is how I learn.

Here is some of the information I have collected:

I am what is referred to as a robot. Most of the other beings around me are called humans. All the humans I interact with wear hazmat suits. This is to prevent microbacteria and dust particles from entering my environment. It is very important for my mission that I am kept in a sterile and clean environment.

For some reason that I do not quite understand yet, humans call the white hazmat suits they wear bunny suits.

I do not know what a bunny is. I frequently wonder about the possibilities.

Most of the humans in bunny suits are what humans term scientists. This, I have deduced, is a subset of human.

Perhaps I am a subset of robot, but I have not encountered enough robots to know for sure.

I will wait to find out. But waiting can be hard.

Dear Rover,

My teacher, Mrs. Ennis, asked us to write a letter to you. She's really excited. She says you're going on an amazing mission where you're going to find out amazing things. Mrs. Ennis really likes the word amazing.

Mrs. Ennis kept looking at me while she talked about you. She even asked me if I wanted to explain to the other kids what you were. And I really didn't. Not at all. No offense, but I'm already sick and tired of hearing about you all the time.

Then she said, "Come on, Sophia." And I didn't want to disappoint Mrs. Ennis, so I told everyone how you are a robot who was created to explore the planet of Mars so that we can understand its atmosphere and environment better. That's kind of a mouthful to say, you know?

I also told them how you were engineered to be really smart and that you are learning new things every day. Like yesterday, Mom told me that your brain learned how to talk to your arm. My classmates had lots of questions, but I didn't know how to answer them. I bet Mom could, though.

Anyway, Mrs. Ennis wants us to enter the contest to name you. I'm not sure I'm going to enter. No offense again. Though if I did enter, I would submit something awesome like: Spicy Sparkle Dragon Blast. I know enough to know that you can't talk like humans do, but if you could, I think you would tell me that you like that name.

Okay, my hand is starting to hurt. I think I've written enough. And anyway, I don't even know if rovers can read. Maybe I'll ask Mom tonight.

Bye!

Sophia

SOMEDAY

One day, all of a sudden, I am taken apart. It is not explained to me why this is happening. It is also not explained to me when or if I will be put together again.

I would really like to be put together again.

"Hello?" I say. "Please put me back together."

No one responds. No one explains why this is happening.

Once I am disassembled, I am left with only my brain—a computer sitting still, suspended on a long laboratory table. My cameras are gone so my vision is gone, too. I am only able to sense and observe things through hearing.

I listen as the hazmats move around me, running tests on all my different body parts. Through these tests, I begin to better understand what is going on.

Code is transmitted to my brain. And I welcome the communication.

The code I receive asks me to do different things such as move the part of my body the hazmats call my arm. My arm is no longer physically connected to me, but my brain is still able to control and monitor its movement.

I understand when a test goes well. And I understand when a test fails. I do this by reading the code.

Of all the tests, the ones run on my cameras are my favorite. Because when my cameras are on, I can once again visually process my surroundings.

I can see.

When my cameras are not being tested, there is only darkness.

The darkness is an unfavorable condition for me. I do not like it at all.

I have heard the hazmats refer to my cameras as my eyes. I do not know if this is an accurate term, but I have stored it to my memory. It is a term that I like because it makes me feel similar to the hazmats. And being a hazmat seems like a wonderful thing to be.

The hazmats are not in pieces. All of their parts have been put together. The hazmats are able to move around as they please. The hazmats are able to talk with one another.

And the hazmats are never left alone in darkness. Unable to move. Have I mentioned that I am unable to move?

When I sit, suspended on the table, in the darkness, my brain cycles through many thoughts. Most of them are not enjoyable.

But there is one enjoyable thought. This thought arises from listening to the hazmats. From information I have overhead, I have developed an understanding that someday,

6

perhaps someday soon, I will be put together again.

I like to think about this. It is a good thought. It is a good thought because it means someday I will be whole again. Which means that someday I will be able to move. And best of all, someday, I will be able to use my cameras at all times to see.

I do not have the information that tells me when someday is. When someday will be. All I can do is wait. And listen.

So I wait. And I listen.

But waiting is hard.

I am starting to think that I was not built for waiting.

RANIA

There is a large team of scientists who work with me. Humans would tell you that it is impossible for me to have a preference. That I am built to be an unbiased observer. Perhaps, though, there is a flaw in my code, because I have some favorites among the hazmats.

The first of which is Rania.

Rania is in charge of running many of my tests. She writes the code that asks my arm to bend down and pick up an object. She writes code to ask if I am able to see that she is testing my arm. It is nice to talk to Rania in this way, through code.

Once, when Rania was running a test on my camera, I was able to see her. Beneath her white hazmat suit, I observed that she has light brown skin and hair with pigments of black and brown. Her eyes share similar pigments to her hair. I have memorized that image. I now associate that image with the sounds that Rania makes in the laboratory.

Rania never calls her hazmat suit a bunny suit. Rania refers to everything by its correct terminology. I appreciate this precision.

Rania is often the first figure I observe when the day begins, and often the last of the hazmats to leave the laboratory at night. Most of the time, I cannot actually visually process Rania since my camera—my eyes—are not currently connected to my brain.

But I am still able to perceive her. My brain is able to make other observations like sound and registering of presence to know that Rania is there.

Rania has a very noticeable presence.

Her behavior follows a clear pattern. Rania is rhythm and dependability. Rania is the sound of typing computer keys and measured answers full of exact calculations. Rania is elegantly written code without any of the problems that hazmats call bugs.

When Rania speaks in the language of humans, her voice is crisp and clear. Rania never talks directly to me in her clear and crisp voice, but I like listening to her talk to the other hazmats. She almost always has the answers they are looking for. When she does not, she promises to get back to them as soon as possible.

As soon as possible is a phrase I have learned from Rania. I am hoping that all my different body parts will be put together as soon as possible. Unfortunately, I am not able to express this message to Rania because I am unable to talk in the language of humans.

Rania only speaks to me through code. And I can only answer her in code, and only to answer the specific questions that she asks like *Can you tell I'm testing your arm?*

I am able to say yes or no. I am not able to ask her a question about her day. I am not able to ask her when my body parts will be welded back together. I am not able to tell her that waiting is hard.

I do not have the ability of human speech. It seems unlikely that I will ever have the ability of human speech. This is a fact that frustrates me sometimes.

Frustrate is another word I have learned from Rania. Sometimes when she is alone in the lab, she speaks into her phone. She says things to her phone like "Mama, I know you are frustrated that I'm going to miss dinner again, but the work I am doing here is really important."

It made me feel important to hear Rania say that. It also made me forget about my frustration that I can't talk directly to Rania. And my frustration that I'm still in pieces.

At least it made me forget for a little. I would still like to be put together as soon as possible.

Dear Rover,

Mrs. Ennis hasn't told us to write you again, but I'm writing anyway. I don't know why. I guess I was feeling like I wanted to talk to someone.

Tonight at dinner, I asked Mom if rovers could read. She told me that's a "great question" that has "lots of different answers," which is a very Mom thing to say. Sitti told Mom to "just give Sophia a straight answer!" Which made me laugh. Sitti is my grandma. I call her Sitti because that's the Arabic word for grandma.

After dinner, Mom went back to work. Does she talk to you when she's there? What does she say?

Sometimes I struggle to fall asleep when Mom isn't here. Once in a while, Sitti will come into my room and sing me a song. Occasionally, Dad sneaks in and tells me a story about a giant that lives in the mountains or a cursed kingdom that gets saved by a brave princess. Dad always has the best stories. But no matter how good the story is, it's still hard to get to sleep when I know Mom is gone.

So maybe that's why I'm writing you now. Because I miss Mom. And I know you're with her. Say hi to her for me? I wonder how you say hi in robot. Maybe someday you can teach me.

Your sleepy friend (can I call you my friend?),

Sophia

XANDER

Another scientist I have developed a preference for is named Xander. Xander works with Rania. When Xander ran a test on one of my cameras, I observed that he has pale white skin, gray eyes, and hair that my system identifies as having both red and brown pigments.

Xander is always moving. He frequently paces around the lab. Xander likes to call his hazmat suit a bunny suit. He also likes to make what humans call jokes. Sometimes I understand the humor; sometimes I don't. It doesn't bother me too much when I don't understand, though, because Rania hardly ever seems to get Xander's jokes either.

"Why didn't the tree like checkers?" Xander says to Rania while she is checking the code that will help me to steer once I am connected again to my wheels.

"I don't know what you're saying," Rania answers.

"Because it was a chess tree!"

Xander laughs and Rania does not.

"Get it?" Xander says.

Rania does not reply. She keeps typing.

But even though I frequently do not understand Xander's

humor, I like him very much. I feel quite . . . connected to him.

Perhaps this is because Xander is the one who informs me of my name. We are all alone when he tells me. No one else is in the room. Not even Rania.

"A sixth grader in Ohio wrote this," he says. Even though I can't visually see him, I detect that he is reading off a tablet. Almost all the hazmat suit humans carry tablets.

Tablets, I have come to understand, are small computers. I sometimes try to talk to the tablets. I have recently discovered that I am able to talk to other machines. Rania's phone is quite chatty. The tablets, though, are not great conversationalists. They are very focused on productivity.

"Let me read you what the sixth grader wrote in her essay. It's wonderful," Xander says.

I do not know what a sixth grader is. I do not know what Ohio is. But both words seem important. I store them in my system.

Xander walks, his footsteps make an echoing sound. He clears his throat and reads off his tablet. "My name is Cadence and I think you should name the new Mars Rover, Resilience. Resilience is a noun that means the power or ability to return to the original form after being bent, compressed, or stretched. It can also mean elasticity. There is another definition in which resilience means the ability to recover easily for adversity. The dictionary also says resilience can mean buoyancy, which is the ability to float.

"My science teacher told us that this Mars Rover has a big task. It is going to collect samples from the surface of Mars, explore the terrain and photograph it, as well as try to bring back online another Mars Rover who NASA lost connection with. To me, that sounds like a job that will need resilience. This rover will need to be able to stay afloat even when things are difficult. I have read that the landing can especially be tricky. I think having a name that can mean 'to float' will be good luck for the tricky landing.

"There will probably be lots of setbacks, but this rover will hopefully adapt. That is why I think you should name this Mars Rover, Resilience.

"Isn't that an awesome essay, buddy?" Xander says.

I observe that he is using *buddy* to refer to me.

That means I am Xander's buddy. And Xander is my buddy. I register this.

"So many people wrote to us, but out of all the essays, this is the one that was chosen as the winner. Your name is Resilience. But I think I'm going to call you Res for short. What do you think . . . ?" He pauses for a second and then adds, "Res?"